CW01197497

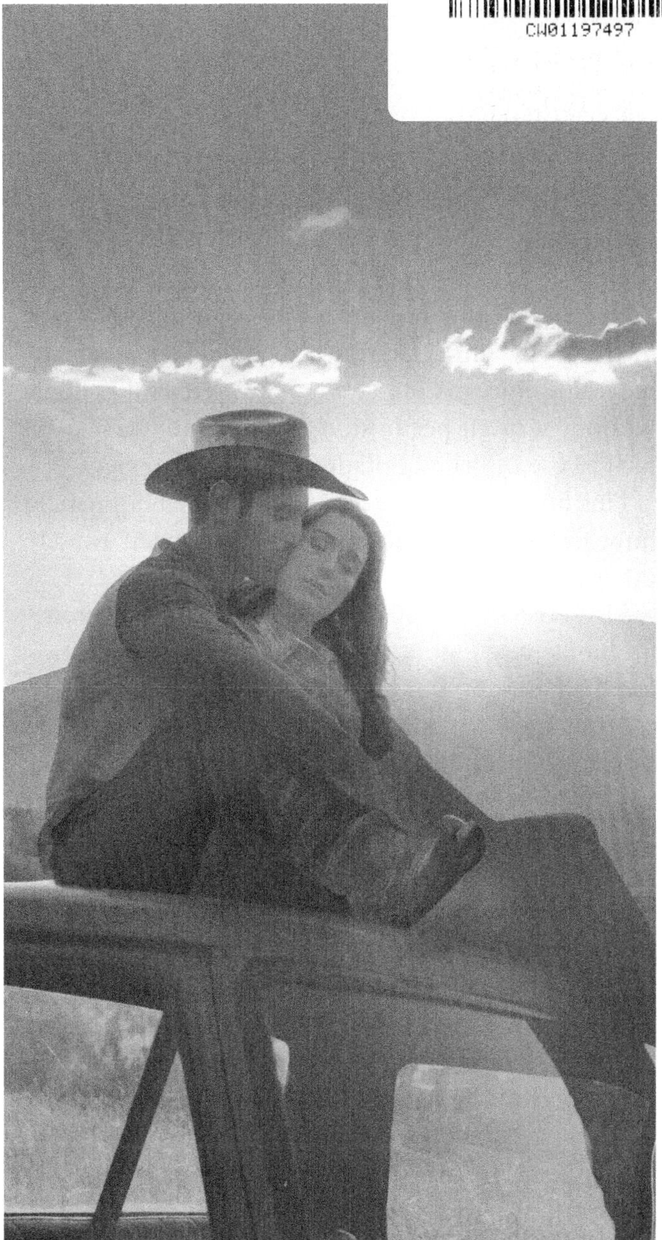

Copyright © 2024 by Jennie Marts
All rights reserved.

No part of this book may be reproduced in any form or by any electronic or mechanical means, including information storage and retrieval systems, without written permission from the author, except for the use of brief quotations in a book review.

This book is licensed for your personal enjoyment only. This book may not be re-sold or given away to other people.

AI RESTRICTION: The author expressly prohibits any entity from using this publication for purposes of training artificial intelligence (AI) technologies to generate text, including without limitation technologies that are capable of generating works in the same style or genre as this publication. The author reserves all rights to license uses of this work for generative AI training and development of machine learning language models.

This book is a work of fiction. Names, characters, places, and incidents are either a product of fiction or are used in a fictitious manner, including portrayal of historical figures and situations. Any resemblance to actual persons living or dead is entirely coincidental.

Cover Design & Interior Format:
The Killion Group, Inc.

SECOND CHANCE WITH A *Cowboy*

LASSITER RANCH

JENNIE MARTS

*This book is dedicated to everyone
who believes in second chances,
in love and in life…
and to those who know that
love's story doesn't always end on the first page…*

*"A second chance isn't about starting over…
it's about continuing the story you were
always meant to tell together."*

CHAPTER ONE

CHEVY LASSITER HAD no idea the surprise he was in store for as a blast of cool air and the scent of coffee and freshly baked pastries hit him as he grudgingly pushed through the door and into the coffee shop at the end of Main Street. He'd spent the last two hours on the tractor bringing in hay from the north pasture, so the air conditioning should have lifted his mood, but he still felt cranky for having to leave the ranch and make the trip into town.

He wouldn't be here at all if he hadn't lost a bet to his brothers. He was way too cheap to pay six dollars for a cup of coffee, when he could make a pot of Folger's at home for less than a nickel a cup.

He looked around and had to admit the space was nice—hardwood floors, soft gray walls, and ambient lighting. A long butcher block-topped bar ran the length of the back of the shop with pastry cases on one side and a huge chalkboard with a hand-lettered menu hung on the wall behind it. The back wall was open on either side, indicating office or storage space behind it.

Everything was either gray, white, or wood-toned with subtle pink and blue accents in the wall art and comfy throw pillows scattered around the furniture. The room was spacious with several small tables and chairs, but the two gray loveseats and a couple of comfy chairs turned toward each other in one corner gave it a cozy homey feel.

He nodded at Judy Fitzgerald, the County Clerk who was tucked into the corner of one of the loveseats and had looked up from the book she was reading to offer him a smile and then gave a wave to Will Perkin's oldest kid—he couldn't remember his name—who was pecking away at his laptop, a huge cup of coffee and a half-eaten Danish on the table beside the computer.

In a town of less than fifteen hundred people, it was rare that Chevy walked into any business and didn't recognize at least some of the people inside.

His phone buzzed as he headed toward the counter, and he pulled it out to see the promised text from his younger brother, Dodge, with their coffee orders.

A copper-haired girl—she looked about fifteen—stood behind the counter and greeted him with a braces-filled smile.

Chevy smiled back. He couldn't remember her name either, but he assumed she was a Johnson—the red hair and freckles giving her away. A person couldn't throw a rock in Woodland Hills or the surrounding county without hitting one of the fair-skinned ginger clan.

"Welcome to Mountain Brew," the girl said,

her perky attitude not enough to change Chevy's annoyed one. "What can I get you?"

"My brothers sent me in. I need some coffee," Chevy said, tapping at his phone to get to Dodge's message.

"You've come to the right place then," she said, her smile firmly in place as she reached to pull a plastic cup from a stack on the counter. "How many drinks do you need?"

"Four, I guess." As long as he was here, he might as well get one for himself too.

"Hot drinks or cold?

"Hot." It was midmorning and already pushing eighty outside, but as far as he was concerned, coffee was meant to be drank hot.

She grabbed a marker and held it poised over the side of the cup. "And what's the name on the first order?"

"Chevy."

She spelled his name out in neat block letters before setting the cup on the counter and reaching for another one.

"Dodge," he told her then waited a beat as she wrote his younger brother's name then reached for another cup. "The next one is Ford."

She lifted the marker and planted the hand holding the cup on her waist. "Is this a joke?"

He assumed she was referring to the names of himself and his brothers. This wasn't the first, nor would it be the last, time he'd been asked that question or taken a ribbing for his and his siblings' names. Their mother, presumably in a drunken state, since that's the state she was usually in, had named him and his two half-brothers after the trucks their dead-beat dads had driven away from her in.

Yeah, Brandy Lassiter, was a real peach. She was also a dirty blonde, a decent singer, and a drunk, who had deposited her three young sons at her parent's ranch and never come back for them. Ford had been used to seeing their mother in an inebriated state—he and Dodge had been too young when she'd left—but now they had no idea what state she was in. But they knew it *wasn't* Colorado. Not in Woodland Hills, at least.

They hadn't seen, or heard from her, in years.

She used to send occasional birthday cards, usually a few weeks after their birthdays, and sometimes with a crumpled five or ten-dollar bill inside. Although one year—he'd probably been eleven or twelve at the time—he'd gotten a card with a twenty. He'd split the money with his brothers since Ford's last card had come with three singles inside.

"Not a joke," he assured the puzzled barista. But these coffee orders surely had to be. He glanced up at the menu board and saw several similarly named items before reading the ones in his brother's message out loud to the girl. "It says Dodge wants a Purple Unicorn Volcano with an extra shot of caffeine, Ford wants a Dragon's Breath Espresso, and Duke wants something called a Caramel Crappuccino."

The girl wrinkled her nose as she wrote each order down on a slip of paper by the register. "I don't recognize these. But I'm pretty new here, and lots of people have specialty drinks." She chewed on her bottom lip as she scanned the orders again. "I think I need to get my manager."

Great. Now this fool's errand would take even longer. Where had these guys even come up with these drinks? He scanned the menu board behind the counter and didn't see the ones they'd named.

The Johnson girl leaned her head around the back wall, presumably calling out to someone with more coffee drink experience. "Hey, can you come out here for a minute? This guy just ordered a Purple Unicorn Volcano and a Caramel Crappuccino, and I don't know how to make either one."

"A Caramel *Crapp*-uccino? Was he serious?" a voice asked from behind the wall.

Everything inside Chevy froze—every muscle, every nerve. His heart might have stopped beating as well.

Even though he hadn't heard it in ten long years, he knew that voice. Knew it as surely as his own.

"Leni?" he tried to say, but it came out as a horse croak.

She walked around the corner—her long, dark hair pulled up in a messy bun and secured with two coffee stir sticks—and his stomach pitched as if he'd just gotten the wind knocked out of him.

She looked almost the same. Although the teenage body of Eleanor 'Leni' Gibbs—which he also knew almost as well as his own—now held the lush curves of a woman. Curves that had him forcing a swallow as his mouth had gone as dry as the hay bales he'd been hauling that morning. She wore a navy apron over a pink polo shirt with the logo of the coffee shop across the breast pocket, white low-top tennies, and ankle-length jeans that hugged her generous hips.

Her eyes were still the same gorgeous, hazel green

and for just one second—long enough for him to feel it to his core—they held the old tenderness he used to see there.

Then it was gone. Replaced with a sharp snap of anger.

He knew that look too.

It was the one she'd given him the night he'd told the biggest lie of his life and said he didn't love her anymore.

He closed his mouth, which had fallen open at the sight of her, then opened it to speak, then closed it again as no words formed. He tried once more, and this time her name came out as a whisper. "Leni?"

Just as quickly as time had frozen for him, it suddenly sped up as blood surged through his veins, and his heart thundered in his chest, like the galloping of a herd of wild stallions. Even his hands started to shake, and he crammed one in his front pocket and gripped his phone tighter with the other.

"Well, as I live and breathe, if it isn't Chevy Lassiter." Her voice held a note of casualness, but he noticed her hand shot out to steady herself against the counter.

Good to know seeing him was having at least *some* effect on her as well.

She jerked her thumb at him as she spoke to the Johnson girl. "Is this the guy with the idiotic drink orders?"

The red-haired girl nodded.

Leni's eyes flashed another spark of anger. "Did you come in here to poke fun at me for working as a barista in a coffee shop?"

Chevy stepped back, his gut aching as if she'd

physically punched him in it. "What? No. Of course not. Why would you even think that?"

"Because you just ordered a Purple Unicorn and a Crappuccino." She jutted out one hip and planted her fist on it. "Is this your lame idea of a joke?"

He hadn't made a joke, but he was beginning to see that he'd been the butt of one. "No, really, it was my stupid brothers. I lost a bet and had to buy coffee—those are *their* idiotic drink orders. Not mine. I didn't even know you were in town."

"Yeah, right. I saw Dodge here just a few days ago. You're trying to tell me he didn't blab to you that I was here?"

"No. He didn't say anything. I swear." But he was going to say a few choice things to his baby brother when he got back to the ranch. "Really. I had no idea you were back."

"I'm not *back*. I'm just filling in here for a few weeks for my sister."

Leni's sister, Lorna Gibbs, now Williams, owned the coffee shop. She'd been a couple of years younger than them in school. He was pretty sure she'd been in Dodge's class, but had seemed older because she'd dated, then married, Lyle Williams, an upperclassman. The two had broken up about nine months ago—it had been ugly with Lyle making an ass of himself then leaving town with the administrative assistant at the insurance company he worked for.

Lorna was left behind with a five-year-old son, a cute kid named Max, and a baby on the way, but she was better off without that jerk in her life.

"Oh yeah, I heard Lorna had a baby girl," Chevy said. "How's she doing?"

"She's fine." Leni's voice was flat, monotone.

"How are *you* doing? I mean, how is your life? Are you happy?"

Are you still single? Please God, don't be married.

His heart wouldn't be able to take it if she were. He snuck a glance at her hand—no ring—and let out a sigh of relief.

"No. You don't get to ask me about *my life*," she said, all monotony gone from her tone, now replaced with a sizzle of anger. "You made it *quite* clear that you didn't want anything to do with me *or* my life. So, you don't get to waltz in here looking all cute and charming in your favorite cowboy hat and start asking questions about *my* life."

"I didn't *mean* to do anything. I just came in for some coffee."

"Well sorry," she said, stacking the cups with their names printed on them and tossing them in the trash. "There's no coffee."

"Wait. What?" The Johnson girl gestured to the large carafe. "I just made a fresh pot."

"It's not for him," Leni told her. "In fact, we're closed." She came out from behind the counter and shooed him with her apron, as if he was a sheep, and she was a border collie herding him toward the corral gate.

The kid at the table in the corner looked up from his laptop. "You're closing?"

"No—not for you," Leni told him, gesturing him back to his computer. "You're fine."

"What about me?" Judy asked, looking up from her book.

"You're fine, too. Everyone can stay. Except him."

She pointed at Chevy then at the front door. "We are closed to you and anyone else named Lassiter." She frowned. "Except for Duke. He can come in. You know, I'd do anything for Duke."

Yeah. Most everyone in town would do anything for his grandfather—including Chevy and his brothers. Duke and June hadn't even hesitated to take in the three boys after their mother had gone to work at the diner one day. It must've been a helluva long shift because she never came back.

"What about the coffee?" Chevy asked, not knowing what else to say. He hadn't expected her to physically push him out of the shop.

"Get it from the gas station," she said, placing one hand on his shoulder and the other on his bare forearm as she propelled him out the door. "Tell Duke I said hi," she said as she pulled the door shut and flipped the sign hanging from it to *Closed*. She gave him a little finger wave as he backed toward his pickup.

What the heck had just happened? He'd imagined running into Leni Gibbs again a hundred different ways, but it had never gone like that, with her closing down a business and shoving him out the door so she wouldn't have to even talk to him.

Still, she was back in town. Close enough that he could figure out how to casually run into her again.

She'd said she was only here for a few weeks to help Lorna, but maybe that was long enough for him to convince her to give him a second chance.

Chapter Two

Fifteen minutes later, Chevy strode into the ranch house to where his brothers and Ford's girlfriend, Elizabeth, sat around the old farmhouse table, and dropped a cardboard holder with four coffees from the gas station secured inside. "Real funny."

Murphy, his English cream golden retriever, sensing his irritation, got up from his bed by the fireplace and ran over to comfort him by rubbing against his legs. Chevy absently reached down to pat the dog's head.

Dodge made a disgusted face at the cups. "Hey, this is from *The Gas and Go*." He offered Chevy an accusatory stare but couldn't hide the glint of amusement in his eyes. "What happened to my Purple Unicorn Volcano?"

"And my Dragon's Breath Expresso?" Ford asked.

"Funny. I figured out your stupid trick," Chevy told them. "Not cool. And I don't think Leni appreciated it either. So, this gas station crap is all you assholes deserve. And I'm not saying I spit in one of those coffees, but I'm not *not* saying it either."

"Who's Leni?" Elizabeth asked, pulling her hand back from the cup she'd been reaching for.

"Oh good, you're back," Duke Lassiter said as he walked in and then paused to hang his cowboy hat on one of the hooks inside the front door. Ford's golden retriever, Dixie, snuck past him before the screen shut and made a beeline for Elizabeth who reached out to scratch the dog's ears. "Did you bring the coffee?"

Chevy turned and offered his grandfather a disgusted sigh. "Come on, Gramps. Not you too? How did these two jokers con you into playing such a dirty trick on me?"

With his thick white beard, handlebar mustache, and the mischievous grin he often wore, Duke looked like a cross between Sam Elliott and Santa Claus. But he wasn't grinning now as he used his thumb and forefinger to smooth his moustache while he gazed around the table at his grandsons. "What dirty trick?"

Chevy narrowed his eyes as he studied him then shook his head. "You *had* to know what was going on. You ordered a caramel *crap*puccino."

His grandfather frowned. "Isn't that what it's called? Those slushy coffee concoctions?"

"No, Duke, they're called *Frap*puccinos," Elizabeth explained with a laugh.

Duke shrugged. "Sounds the same to me." He pulled one of the cups from the cardboard holder, took a sip, then grimaced before setting it back down and heading into the kitchen.

Murphy followed him in, just in case he was planning to offer him a treat or drop any food on the floor. Used to having the golden retrievers around him, Duke maneuvered around the dog as he picked up the carafe from the ancient Mr. Coffee that had sat on the counter for the last twenty years and carried it to the sink. "I'll make us some real coffee while you all tell me about this dirty trick you played on your brother."

"It wasn't that dirty," Ford said, ruffling his dog's neck. She was splitting her attention between him and Elizabeth, pushing her head against Ford's hand for pets while jostling her rump against Elizabeth for scratches. "The time we put the frogs in his bed—now *that* was dirty."

Elizabeth made a disgusted face as Ford and Dodge cracked up.

"This was all in good fun," Dodge said. "We knew Leni was back in town and filling in for her sister at the coffee shop, and we just thought it would be a good way for Chevy to…" He used his fingers to make air quotes. "… '*accidentally*' run into her."

"Wait," Duke said, pausing in between dumping another scoop of ground coffee into the filter. "Leni is back? Leni Gibbs?"

Elizabeth let out an exasperated sigh. "Would somebody *please* tell me who Leni Gibbs is?"

Ford pulled one of the cups from the carton, apparently not too concerned by his brother's threat that he'd spit in one, because he took a long gulp, grimaced worse than his grandfather had, then chugged down half the cup. "Leni Gibbs was the love of Chevy's life," he explained as he wiped his mouth on the side of his sleeve.

"She was the one who got away," Dodge added.

"She didn't *get away*," Ford corrected. "Chevy *pushed* her away."

Elizabeth's brows drew together. "Why?"

"Because he's a dumb ass," Ford said.

She ignored his comment. "Because he didn't really love her?"

"No," Duke said. "Because he loved her so much that he let her go." He brought a set of cups out, his thumbs threaded through their handles. They clinked as he set them on the table. "Leni was a real smart girl—still is, I presume—she had several colleges lined up, most of them offering her scholarships. Big ones."

"Big schools or big scholarships?" Elizabeth asked.

"Both," Chevy answered softly, his gaze focused on the coffee mug he'd picked up. Murphy had given up on getting a treat and come back to lay on the floor, his body sprawled across Chevy's boots, ready to offer emotional support when needed. "She got a big offer from MIT, a place she'd dreamed of going since we were kids."

"That sounds amazing," Elizabeth said.

"It was," Dodge told her. "But she and Chevy had finally gotten together—after being friends for years, but really in love with each other forever."

"That sounds nice," Elizabeth said, but the miserable look on Chevy's face showed it was anything but.

"She wanted to give up MIT and stay in Woodland Hills," Ford said. "For Chevy."

Chevy set the cup down, but his gaze remained on it. "And I couldn't have her give up everything she'd ever dreamed of. Not for someone like me."

"I don't know what that means," Elizabeth said. "You're a great guy."

"Thanks. You're sweet," Chevy said. This is why

everyone in the family had fallen in love with Elizabeth almost as much as Ford had. She had a way of looking on the bright side and always seemed to have a kind word for everyone. "But it doesn't matter how great I was. I couldn't let her give up everything—her chance at an awesome college, a bright future, an amazing career. So, I tried to break it off."

"But she didn't believe him. Or she wouldn't accept it," Dodge said. "Even though he tried to break up with her like four times. So, he finally had to 'Old Yeller' her."

Elizabeth looked from one brother to the other. "Old Yeller her? I don't get it. She had rabies so he had to take her out back and shoot her?"

Dixie let out a whine and snuggled closer to Ford.

Dodge laughed. "Oh, maybe I got that wrong. But you know, whatever that movie was where the kid tries to get the dog to leave, but the dog won't go because he loves the kid so much, so he starts yelling at it, telling the dog he doesn't care about it anymore, and that he never did. Then he picks up a rock and throws it at him to get him to leave."

Elizabeth raised an eyebrow at Chevy. "You threw a rock at this girl?"

Chevy shook his head as he let out a huff. "No, of course not. But I did do all that other stuff. Told her I didn't love her and that I never had."

Elizabeth's shoulders sank, and her tone softened. "Oh, Chevy."

"Hardest thing I ever had to do. Broke both our hearts and any kind of relationship we would ever be able to have again." He let out a weary sigh then buried his head in his hands. "But I had to. She wouldn't have left otherwise."

"That's ancient history, brother. She told me she was here for at least a few weeks while she helps her sister with the new baby," Dodge said. "So, what are you going to do to win her back?"

Chevy lifted his head and stared at Dodge. "Who says I want to win her back?"

They all just stared at him for a few seconds then Dodge, in a soft voice, finally said, "Bro."

Chevy let out a hard breath. "Okay. Yeah, I'm gonna try to win her back."

Elizabeth clapped her hands. "Yay. What can we do to help?"

Chapter Three

That afternoon, Leni stomped into her sister's house—the same yellow one they'd grown up in at the end of Aspen Grove Lane—slammed the door behind her and dumped her purse and tote bag on the counter, knocking into a glass and sloshing water onto the counter.

Her younger sister, Lorna looked up from the kitchen table where she was coaxing green beans into her five-year-old son's mouth and gently shaking baby Isabel in her bouncy seat in the center of the table. Lorna and her kids favored their mom's side of the family, fair skin and smooth blond tresses, so different from Leni, who had inherited their father's wavy dark hair.

"Wow," Lorna said, her eyes wide as she watched her sister grab a paper towel and furiously wipe at the spill. "Who pooped in your Fruit Loops?"

Her five-year-old, Max, covered a giggle with his hand. "You said *poop*."

"I think the correct saying is who *peed* in your Froot Loops," Leni corrected with a snarl.

Max giggled again. "Pee."

"Yes, I know the correct saying," her sister said, unfazed by Leni's growly correction. "But your current mood seemed to call for an adjective stronger than merely pee-soaked cereal."

Max couldn't take it. His giggles overtook him as he flung himself down on the padded bench seat, the green beans forgotten, as he succumbed to a fit of laughter.

"So, are you gonna tell me what's got you so worked up?" Lorna asked with a quick grin at her giggling son before returning her attention to her sister.

Leni's shoulders slumped as she sank into the empty chair at the table. "I saw him today."

"How was it?" her sister asked, neither one of them having to explain or elaborate on who the "him" was.

"Oh, about like you'd expect. And nothing like the way I'd envisioned it happening in any of the many scenarios I've imagined in the past decade. He, of course, still looked hot as hell…" She cast a quick glance at her nephew who was trying to catch his breath from laughing so hard. "Sorry, I mean hot as *heck*. I'm sure you've seen him around, so you know, same dark hair, same tall, lean build, except now his shoulders are a million times broader, and he's gotten ten times more muscles than he had as a teenager. His smile was the same though. At one point, he grinned at me, just like he used to, and I swear, my knees went so wobbly I had to grab the counter for support." She let out a sigh. "I've always hoped I would run into him when I was looking my best, with my hair curled and all decked out in a cute outfit, or at least wearing something more than just a swipe of mascara and a polo shirt with a coffee stain on the front." She groaned. "I didn't even wash my hair this morning."

"Don't worry about that," her sister said. "You still look amazing. And you're way prettier now than you were in high school."

"Thanks," she deadpanned. "That means a lot... coming from my *sister*."

"So, what did you do?" Lorna asked, ignoring the gibe.

"What do you think I did? I acted all cool, like seeing him didn't bother me a bit." She crossed her arms on the table and groaned again as she leaned her forehead against them. "Then I told him we were closed and kicked him out of the coffee shop."

"Solid move. Did you kick the other customers out too? Assuming there were other customers."

"Yes, there were. And don't worry, I let them stay. But knowing this town, everyone's already heard how I shoved Chevy Lassiter out the front door of the coffee shop and flipped the closed sign in his face."

"Wish I could've been there."

"Yeah, I wish you would've been there too. I'm sure you would have handled it better."

Lorna shrugged. "Maybe. But I see him all the time. And of course, I'm always going to be in your corner—Team Leni, and all that—but I still kind of like the guy. He's just fun to be around. And he's nice. A few weeks before Izzy was born, he and his family were sitting in the pew in front of us at church, and Max went up to sit with them. He took his crayons and a coloring book, and Chevy colored with him during the whole sermon."

Leni swallowed. She didn't want to hear about what

a great guy Chevy Lassiter was. He'd broken her heart and almost destroyed her. It was bad enough that she had to see him today and was almost crushed by the weight of all the feelings she apparently still had for him. "*Why* are you telling me this?"

Lorna nudged Max back into a sitting position and gestured toward the remaining three green beans and the last chicken nugget on his plate. "I don't know. Because you cared so much about him, and it seems like maybe you still do. And he just seems nice, so maybe he's changed."

"*Changed*? A wolf doesn't change into a golden retriever." She let out a huff as she crossed her arms over her chest. "You know what he did to me, right?"

"Yes. I know he broke your heart and told you he didn't love you anymore."

"That wasn't all he did."

"What do you mean?"

She loosened her arms and picked up a napkin from the table. Holding it in her lap, she stared down at it, her voice going quieter as she told her sister, "He didn't *just* break up with me. He also left me for someone else."

Lorna's eyes widened as she jerked her head back. "Wait. You never told me this."

"Because I was embarrassed and humiliated."

"Are you sure? I've been in town this whole time, and I've never seen Chevy dating anyone seriously since you left. Who was it?"

"I don't know. Some bimbo named *Jolene*."

"Like the song?" Lorna started humming the chorus of the Dolly Parton tune.

Leni held up her hand. "Yes. Stop. Please. It already

feels like a cliché." Although she couldn't help pressing her hand to her heart and belting out for Jolene to please not take her man.

Lorna frowned. "Are you for real right now? Someone named Jolene really stole Chevy from you that summer?"

"I don't think she stole him. It seems like he went willingly, because he told me he'd given his heart to someone new."

"He said that?" Lorna wrinkled her nose as if she'd just smelled a dirty diaper.

"Yep. He told me she needed him more, and he was going to give her all his attention."

"I'm sorry. I honestly don't know anything about another girl. I don't even *know* anyone named Jolene. But I'm sure they're not together now."

"Like I care."

"It seems like you do."

"I don't."

Lorna's expression softened, and she put her hand on her sister's shoulder. "I'm sorry. I know Chevy broke your heart."

"No," Leni said, the napkin now a pile of shreds in her lap. "He broke *me*. You know, I haven't had one serious relationship since being with him. He ruined me for anyone else."

"Okay. Yes, I know. But really, you have to admit, he actually did you a favor."

Leni stared at her sister like she'd grown two heads as she choked out, "A *favor*?"

"Yes." She held up her hands in defense. "Don't hate me. But we both know that if he hadn't broken up with you, you never would've gone to MIT, or graduated at the top of your class, or earned that fancy aerospace engineering degree that you'd dreamed of getting since you were a little girl. You've created a successful career for yourself in a field you love. And now you've been offered your dream job with NASA. And *none* of that would've happened if you would've stayed behind in Woodland Hills."

Leni nodded grudgingly.

What her sister said was true.

But what did any of that—a fancy degree or a great job—matter if she didn't have the person she loved to share it with.

That night, Chevy galloped toward the barn, both he and his horse breathing hard. He'd pushed her, charging flat out across the back pasture, racing the sun setting behind the mountain, and trying to outrun all the feelings seeing Leni Gibbs had dredged up in him again.

Murphy ran to greet them as they trotted into the farmyard. The dog had just turned twelve and couldn't always keep up when Chevy took long rides up into the mountains, although he loved to try.

Climbing down from the saddle, Chevy greeted the dog then led the horse to the spicket just outside the barn door. Turning on the faucet, he splashed his face and head then cupped his hands to take a drink of the cool water before it filled the rubber horse bucket on the ground below.

The horse dipped her head and took a long drink then nuzzled into Chevy's shoulder.

He put his arm around her and returned the affection, brushing his hand down her long velvety neck then giving her flank a pat. The familiar scents of dry straw, leather, and old wood met him as he entered the barn and led her back to her stall. His voice was low, talking to her as he often did while he brushed and groomed her.

She stamped and occasionally swished her tail as if in response. The horse was a good listener. And a good friend.

She'd been a colt when he'd gotten her from a neighboring ranch a decade ago. Her mother, a sweet mare, had died in childbirth and the rancher, a good friend of Duke's, had sold the foal to Chevy for a song, knowing the teenager was going to have to bottle feed her for the first three months of her life.

Duke liked to say that Chevy had saved the foal's life, but he knew the truth. The colt had saved him. He'd been heartbroken and depressed that summer, but caring for the baby horse, bottle-feeding it every three or four hours, weighing it, tracking its growth and progress, kept him distracted and his mind off constantly thinking about the girl he'd pushed away.

Leni Gibbs had meant everything to him, and he'd loved her with everything he had. But he knew then, just like he knew now, he wasn't the guy anyone stuck around for. Not his dad. Not even his own mother. Leni was too smart, too driven. She had big dreams, and he knew if she stayed in Woodland Hills, for him, she'd either resent him later or eventually leave him anyway.

It was easier…no, not *easier*…but *better* the way he'd done it. She might not ever forgive him, but he would know, in his heart, that he'd done the right thing. For her.

If you love something, let it go…and all that crap. Still hurt though.

He pulled the brush down the horse's chestnut brown neck, trying to push aside the memories of that summer.

Finished with her grooming, he filled the horse's trough with fresh hay and let her nibble a couple of sugar cubes from his palm, before closing her stall door and giving her ears one last scratch.

He whistled for the dog then called over his shoulder to the horse as he left the barn, "Good night, Jolene."

Chapter Four

Leni juggled two gallon cartons of coffee and a box of pastries as she traversed the steps leading into the basement of the Presbyterian Church. It had been three days since she'd seen Chevy—and about three *minutes* since she'd last thought about him.

He hadn't been back into the coffee shop or tried to reach out to her. Although, why would he after the way she'd kicked him out the last time he'd been there?

She should have been too busy to think about him. She'd been putting in long hours at Mountain Brew and helping her sister with the kids. Isabel had been up four times the night before, and the lack of sleep was getting to all of them.

But the whole reason she'd come back to Woodland Hills was to help her sister in her time of need. So, she'd gotten up early to take care of Izzy and get Max ready and given her sister a few extra hours to sleep before she'd left for work.

They'd been trying to hire another barista, but the application pool had been thin so far. Leni knew if the shop were taken care of, it would allow her sister to worry less and be able to just focus on Max and Izzy. Which was why she'd been trying to branch out the shop's take-out services and making this delivery herself. She hoped the word would spread and more people would order coffee and pastries for their meetings and get-togethers.

This delivery was for the women of *Knitty Gritty*—a knitting circle that had been meeting in the church basement for as long as Leni could remember.

Walking down the stairs, she was overwhelmed with memories of spending so much time here as a kid. This had been the church she and her mom and Lorna had come to since they'd moved to Woodland Hills when she was twelve. She'd been surprised at the way they'd embraced a single mom with two young daughters, and this basement had been where she'd first met Chevy and his brothers. She remembered sitting next to the tall, skinny kid with the lock of dark hair—so different from his blond brothers— that always seemed to be falling into his eyes. She inhaled as she stepped into the room. It still smelled the same—old wood, dusty hymnals, worn carpet, and the lingering scents of past potlucks.

This is why she had avoided coming back to Woodland Hills. Everywhere she turned was a memory of the boy who had broken her heart.

Three round tables had been set up in the center of the room, piles of yarn and knitting bags with needles sticking out of their tops covered the middle of each. Sounds of laughter filled the room, and Leni was surprised that the number of women in the group had grown instead of dwindled and that there were quite a few younger women in the group as well.

She'd heard knitting was good for stress. Maybe she'd have to look into it.

Yeah, because she didn't already have enough on her plate. She should for sure take up a needlework craft.

She recognized several of the older women sitting together at a large table near the kitchen. Ruby Foster, Greta Newton, and Mabel Turner were all in their eighties and pillars of their small-town community. The woman had been best friends most of their lives, along with Chevy's grandmother, June, who had passed away several years before.

Grr. Now she was thinking about Chevy *again*. She couldn't even deliver coffee to a bunch of old ladies without somehow connecting her thoughts back to that man.

"Hi Miss Ruby," Leni said, pushing away the memories of the cute cowboy as she held up the cartons of coffee. "Where do you want these?"

"Well, I'll be," Ruby said, getting up from the table and coming around to hug her, which wasn't an easy feat considering she was holding two gallons of coffee and a box of baked goods. "Eleanor Gibbs, how good to see you. I heard you were back in town. How's Lorna doing?"

"Not *back*," she corrected. "Just here for a few weeks to help my sister. And she and the baby are doing great."

"You tell her we're all itching to cuddle that sweet baby, and we've got the nursery ready for Isabel when Lorna's feeling up to coming back to church," Greta said, her hands busy weaving yarn around two long knitting needles.

"You're welcome to come with her," Mabel added. "Whenever you like."

"Thank you. I appreciate it. For now, I'd better just get this coffee set up for you all and get back to the shop."

"You can take it into the kitchen," Ruby told her. "We've got some trays already set up in there."

She turned toward the kitchen. Then her mouth fell open as a tall dark-haired man, who had a frilly pink apron wrapped around his waist, walked out carrying a tray filled with white cups and small matching saucers.

Ruby leaned in to whisper, "Close your mouth, dear. Or you're bound to catch flies."

Leni snapped her mouth closed. Then opened it again to sputter, "What are you doing here?"

"It's Thursday morning. I'm here for knitting club," Chevy said, matter-of-factly as he set the tray on a rectangle table near her.

"You *knit?*"

"Not very well," Mabel said, pointing to a crumpled mass of yarn sitting next to a leather saddlebag. "He's a bit hopeless when it comes to the knitting part—he's been working on the same scarf for the past two years."

"He's better at frogging than knitting," Greta added with a good-natured chuckle.

Leni stared at the bundle of blue yarn that in no way resembled a scarf. "Frogging?"

"It's called frogging when you unravel or rip out stitches to fix a mistake," Chevy explained. "You know, like *rip it, rip it,*" he said, mimicking the sound made by a frog.

Leni just blinked at him. Was this really happening? She'd only seen Chevy once in the last decade, and now he was standing in front of her wearing a pink apron and croaking like a bull frog.

"But we wouldn't get here at all if he didn't pick us up every other Thursday and bring us to the church. He's kind of like our *Knitty Gritty* mascot," Mabel said.

"And we all usually have a list of things we need his help with once he drops us off," Greta said. "Which reminds me, Chevy, honey, I think I accidentally signed out of Netflix again yesterday. Will you take a look at my remote this afternoon and see if you can fix it?"

Chevy ducked his head. "Of course, Miss Greta."

"He takes pretty good care of us old gals," Ruby said, then winked at Leni as she gestured toward the other tables. "And our group numbers have certainly risen since he's been in attendance."

Ah. It suddenly made sense why there were more younger women in the group. And Leni assumed most of them were single. And probably looking to catch a hunky bachelor who knitted and carted old ladies around after fixing their Netflix accounts.

"We've got plenty of yarn," Ruby said, gesturing to the assorted colors of skeins on the table. "And we could always use another member, if you want to give it a try."

Leni shook her head. "Thanks, but my fingers need the rest when they're not clicking away at my computer keyboard. Or using my newfound barista skills. I just came by to personally deliver the coffee and baked goods and to say that I hope you think of Mountain Brew coffee for all your meetings and events."

"We're glad you called us," Greta told her. "I didn't even know you *could* buy coffee by the gallon, but we're delighted to be able to support Lorna. We'd like to set this up as a regular thing and have coffee and pastries delivered to all our meetings." She waved a hand toward Ruby. "You can fix it all up with Ruby. Our little club has plenty of dues to use, and she's our self-designated treasurer."

"That sounds amazing," Leni said, thrilled that her idea would bring in a consistent sale for the coffee shop.

"I'll call you later this week to iron out the details," Ruby said, then gestured toward the kitchen. "For now, why don't you and Chevy get us all set up, before that delicious smelling coffee gets cold."

"Yes, ma'am," Chevy said, taking one of the cartons of coffee from her then holding the kitchen door open for Leni to walk through.

"Nice apron," she told him as the door swung shut behind them, trying not to be distracted by that same shock of dark hair that still fell across his forehead.

He chuckled. "Thanks. I'm not sure pink is my best color, but those old gals sure get a kick out of it when I put this on. And it's fun to make them laugh."

"You always did like to be the center of attention." Her tone was a little harsher than she'd intended.

Or was it?

It had been ten years. And they'd been in high school. She should be over it by now. But he'd broken her.

And apparently, she was still pissed.

"The curse of the middle child," he agreed, flashing her a grin that once would have made her knees buckle—okay, so maybe it still made her knees a little wobbly—seemingly unfazed by her tone as he pointed to the two cut-glass serving plates and three white thermal carafes set up on a tray. "I can pour the coffee into the carafes if you want to arrange the baked goods. I'm no good at that. I usually just dump them on the plate."

She set the box of pastries and the other gallon carton on the counter next to the trays. "It's got a spigot on it, so they can just pour it right from the carton."

"I know. But they kind of like the whole formal coffee set up. Then it seems like they're having a tea party while they're knitting. It's their thing." He unscrewed the lid and carefully poured coffee into the first carafe. "They're all about tradition, so I'm kind of surprised they agreed to have coffee delivered. I'm glad it's going to work out for Lorna to make this a regular thing though."

"Me too. I wasn't sure when I called them, but apparently, I can be pretty persuasive."

He laughed. "I remember."

She pulled her head back. "Why are you laughing?"

"I was just thinking about the time you talked the school librarian into letting us use the library for a silent disco during our lunch break as a way to make reading seem more cool."

She smiled before she could stop herself. "That was a fun day. Remember how Colt James tried to teach us that coordinated line dance, but we were all listening to different songs?"

Chevy laughed again. "I'd forgotten about that. But I do remember him trying to sneak a goat into the dance and the librarian losing her mind. Remember she was trying to shoo it out with a broom, and it kept trying to eat the bristles?"

Leni cracked up. "She kept yelling, *no goats in the library*. And *don't let it eat the books. Goats love paper.*" She held her stomach. "That was so funny. Did we ever figure out why Colt even had a goat at school?"

He shook his head, still laughing. "Who knows. But I'm not sure your idea convinced anyone to read more."

"No, but it was worth a try," she told him as their laughter died down.

"And it was hilarious." He finished filling one of the carafes and screwed the lid down. "You always had fun ideas."

She laughed again, but this time more wryly. "You and my sister were the only ones who ever thought any of my ideas were *fun*. Everyone else just thought I was a big nerd. Or never thought of me at all."

He kept his gaze on the second carafe as he poured in the last of the liquid from the carton. "I thought about you all the time."

Chapter Five

THE LAUGHTER DIED in Leni's throat, and she suddenly had a hard time swallowing.

"What are you doing here?" she asked him, stiffening her tone as she tried to change the subject. There was no point dredging up old memories from the past.

Those days were gone.

"I'm just pouring coffee," Chevy said. "I told you, the ladies like things fancy."

"No. I mean what are you doing at a knitting club?"

His lips pulled up in a sheepish grin as he lifted his shoulders in a small shrug. "I used to bring my grandma into town for this. Sometimes I'd run errands while I waited to pick her up or I'd just wait in the truck, but she'd usually talk me into coming in and visiting with her and her friends. I'd heard knitting was a good stress reliever, so I gave it a try. I was shit at knitting, but it sure made Gran happy."

She wanted to ask him what he was so stressed about, but he seemed lost in the memory of spending time with his grandmother.

"After a while, I started picking up the other

ladies," he continued. "Ruby, Greta, and Mabel—it just became something they counted on. I went in to help Greta *one* time with her computer, she'd gotten herself locked out of some app or something, and then they *all* started having me help them with stuff. They're pretty independent, but they seem to like having me fuss over them a little bit, and I don't mind helping them out."

"I'll bet," she said, her tone taking on that harshness again. "I'm sure you just love all the attention of these women fussing over you like a bunch of knitting mother hens."

He shrugged, his focus still on the coffee, but his voice was softer now. "Yeah. Actually, I do. Of course I do. You know I had a shit mother, and the only woman who ever treated me like her own was my grandma. And she's gone now. So, yeah, I let my grandmother's best friends' fuss over me a bit. I won't deny that it feels nice to have them spoil me a little, but I spoil them too."

She ducked her head, regretting the roughness of her words. "I'm sorry about June. I wanted to come back for her funeral, but I was in the middle of my master's, and I'd just been offered the job with Boeing…it's not an excuse…I just couldn't make it work."

"It's okay. I understand. Your school and work took priority. And that's how it should be." He nudged her shoulder gently with his. "And she knew you loved her."

"I really did," she whispered, her voice obstructed by the giant lump in her throat. She blinked back the tears that threatened her eyes. She would *not* cry in front of Chevy.

"So," Chevy said, busying himself with the last carafe of coffee. He cleared his throat, as if the mention of his grandmother's funeral stirred emotions in him, too. Or maybe it was talking about her being at school—but that had been *his* choice. "Did you take the job with Boeing?"

"Oh, um, yeah."

"What do you do there?"

"I'm an aerospace engineer."

"Wow. Impressive. So, what do you actually *do*?"

She shrugged, always a little self-conscious talking about her work. When most people found out what she did, they usually either assumed her job was high-powered and like an episode of Top Gun—it was not—or that she was a super-smart boring math and physics nerd. The second one was closer to the truth. "I do a lot of things, but mainly I design, develop, and help test aircraft, satellites, and spacecraft."

That was the part that usually had someone's eyes glaze over with boredom, but Chevy's eyes widened, and a huge grin broke across his face. "That's amazing. Just like you always dreamed of." He reached out like he was going to touch her arm, then must have changed his mind and let his hand drop. His voice was thick with emotion as he told her, "I'm so damn proud of you."

She stared at him, staggered by the sudden well of tears in his eyes, and once again, blinking back her own.

Turning away, she tried to concentrate on setting out the last of the cinnamon buns. "I assumed you knew all this. My sister acts like she brags me about me all the time. And I know you see her here at church." This was a small town. She figured everyone knew exactly what she did. Although, she'd been a nerdy nobody when she'd lived here, and no one had cared about what she did back then, so why would anyone care about what she did now.

Chevy picked up the tray. "Everyone knows what I did, so nobody really talks to me about you," he said before pushing through the door.

"Oh," she said to the empty room, then followed him out with the tray of baked goods. She set them on the table next to the coffee carafes then couldn't figure out what to do with her hands.

"This all looks wonderful," Ruby said, picking up a cheese Danish. "And the coffee smells amazing."

"I hope you all enjoy it," Leni said, trying to get back into business mode. "And speaking of coffee, I should probably get back to the shop. I'll call you tomorrow, Miss Ruby, to follow up on your next order. You all can let me know if there was anything you particularly enjoyed or if there were things you'd rather I leave off next time."

"Sounds good," Greta said, perusing the tray of goodies. "But they all look delicious. I'm sure we're going to enjoy them all."

"Okay, then," she said, backing toward the stairs. "I'll talk to you soon."

"I'll walk you out," Chevy said, untying the apron and leaving it on one of the tables.

"It's okay. You don't have to."

"I know, but I want to."

In truth, she was glad to have him walk her out to her car. As much as she'd dreaded seeing him, now she didn't feel quite ready to say goodbye. Her emotions flip-flopped from happy to sad to angry like a fresh trout caught and released onto the bank of a mountain stream.

As she followed him up the stairs and out into the late summer sunshine, memories flooded through her. They had practically grown up together and reminders of time spent with him were everywhere.

He had hurt her so badly. But it also felt good. Talking and even laughing with him—things she'd been sure would never happen again—felt natural, even a little good, like slipping on one of Chevy's favorite faded flannel shirts again.

He came to an abrupt stop, and she ran into the back of him. Putting her hands up, she couldn't help but notice the solid muscle of his back. Heat warmed her chest as the scent of him surrounded her—the same woodsy cologne with a hint of citrus he'd always worn.

How could accidentally bumping into him bring up so many feelings? Feelings she'd spent years trying to bury.

"Whoa. Is this your car?" He let out a low whistle as he admired her Tesla Model S. "I mean this *must* be your car. I don't think we have another Tesla in town and none with Washington plates. Damn. Boeing must be treating you right. This thing is fancy as all get out."

She pushed back her shoulders, ready to defend the sporty car. They weren't a novelty around Seattle. And she loved the Deep Blue Metallic color but hadn't thought about how much it would stand out in the small mountain town that had mainly trucks and

SUVs parked along the main street of downtown.

"Yes, it's mine. Obviously. But I mainly drive it to help the environment," she told him. Which was true, but she also loved everything else about the car—it's sleek aerodynamic design, the gorgeous gray leather interior, the way the steering wheel and dash had the feel of a luxury spacecraft. "It's all electric, so I'm leaving less of a carbon footprint. And I save a ton by not buying gas and just plugging it in." She didn't need to mention that she'd spent a small fortune buying the car, but she'd used her first bonus at Boeing for the down payment and hadn't ever regretted the decision.

"Wait. No gas at all?" He scratched the back of his neck as he walked around the back of the car as if looking for an outlet. "I hate to sound like a country bumpkin, but I honestly don't know much about these things. You really just plug this car in? To what?"

She tried to hide her smile. Chevy was no country bumpkin. He was just a truck guy. She wondered if he had the same Chevy pickup he'd been driving when she'd last seen him. All the Lassiter brothers drove the brands of truck they were named for. Or at least they had the last time she'd lived here.

"To a charging station," she explained. "It takes between six and twelve hours to fully charge it when I'm at home, but I can do it in less than thirty minutes if I plug into a Supercharger in the city. Then I can get up to two hundred miles in a fifteen-minute charge."

"Really?" He ran his hand along the hood, as if you were itching to pop it and check out the engine.

She nodded. "The only problem here is that our

old house, I mean Lauren's place now, isn't wired for charging it. And the only two places progressive enough in Woodland Hills to even have electric car chargers are the library and the new *Gas and Go* out by the highway—but neither have the Supercharger kind."

"So, how are you charging this thing?"

"At the library. I talked to the librarians, and they said barely anyone uses their charger, so they let me plug it in and leave it there overnight when I first got to town. Like everything in this town, it's only a ten-minute walk away, and I just picked it up on my way to work the next morning."

"Nice. I've never ridden in a Tesla before," he told her, a boyish grin creasing his face. "Maybe I can talk you into giving me a ride in it sometime?"

She shrugged. "I don't know. Maybe." They'd been talking and getting along okay, but that didn't mean she was ready to hop in the car and start cruising around town with him again.

"Remember how we used to drive around town and down all those back country roads? We spent hours in my old truck."

She remembered. Although she remembered more of the times they'd *parked* for hours.

Chevy Lassiter might have broken her heart, but he was a dang great kisser.

He studied her, almost as if he knew exactly what she'd been thinking. "You look good," he said, reaching up to gently tug at one of her curls. "I like your hair longer like this. You look more grown up."

She swallowed, her whole body warming at the softest touch of his hand as his fingers brushed her shoulder. She had been taking a little extra time to get ready in the morning, dusting on a little eye shadow and throwing her hair up into hot rollers and letting it set while she got dressed or adding a few twisted curls with her flat iron after she'd blow-dried it out.

She refused to admit she was taking the extra time with her appearance in case she ran into Chevy—but who was she kidding? Of course she was.

"That's because I *am* a grown up," she told him, pushing her shoulders back then yanking the car door open.

He dropped his gaze. "Yeah, sorry, I didn't mean anything. I just…it's good to see you." He lifted his head, catching her with a look that she couldn't read. "Do you know how long you're going to be in town?"

Her anger flared. She was mad at him for breaking up with her all those years ago and mad at herself for still caring. She narrowed her eyes. "Why? Are you dying to get rid of me already?"

Chevy shook his head, his expression sincere. "I just want to know how much time I have to try to get you to forgive me."

She huffed out a sardonic laugh. "Not enough time in the world."

She got into the car and forced herself not to look in the rearview mirror as she drove away.

Chapter Six

DON'T DO IT, man. Not again.

Chevy told himself not to, but he couldn't help it.

The town of Woodland Hills was laid out in a long rectangle with the streets running longwise named for native trees, Aspen Grove Lane, Blue Spruce Street, Ponderosa Pine Avenue, Juniper Way, and Douglas Fir Drive, intersected by numbered streets.

Main Street ran through the middle of downtown with a courthouse in the center and the businesses fanning out in the blocks surrounding it. The houses and neighborhoods filled either side of the downtown area, with the larger more upscale homes built into the forested areas closer to the mountainside.

Aspen Grove Lane was named for the long band of aspen trees that ran along the creek behind the houses, including the yellow one toward the end of the lane where Chevy knew Leni was staying.

He tried to drive past her street. But it was as if the truck had a mind of its own, and suddenly his blinker was on, and he was turning the steering wheel. Just like he'd done the night before and the night before that.

He was completely conflicted—one minute feeling like a lovesick teenager driving by his crush's house and hoping to catch a glimpse of her in the yard or through the window, the next feeling like a pervy creep driving down his crush's street and hoping to catch a glimpse of her in the yard or through the window.

The night before, the house had been dark, except for one of the upstairs windows. The window used to be Leni's room, but he wasn't sure if Lorna had kept it for her. He knew Lorna and Max had moved back in with her mom after that jackass, Lyle, had left them. But then, during the middle of Lorna's pregnancy, her and Leni's mom had decided to remarry and move to Florida with her new husband, leaving Lorna the house.

The upstairs window gave off a soft glow, and he imagined Leni inside, tucked in bed, wearing a big T-shirt and fuzzy socks—because her feet were always cold. She'd be leaning against the headboard, her nose in a book, oblivious to the time, absorbed in some story.

Or the room could belong to Max now or have been turned into a nursery. Or Lorna could have taken it when Leni left, and she had the light on because she was up with the baby.

It was earlier tonight than it had been when he'd driven by the night before. The clock on his dash read a little past eight, so the sun had just set, but it was still light enough to see. But tonight, there was no soft glow of lamp light.

Instead, the flash of red and blue strobe lights pulsed through the dusky sky.

Chevy's heart raced as he got closer, then stopped altogether when he realized the ambulance and a firetruck were parked in front of Lorna's house.

He slammed on the brakes as he jerked the wheel to the right, almost jumping the curb in his haste to park. He threw the truck in park, cut the engine, and scrambled from the cab, almost tripping over a small yellow dump truck that had been forgotten on the sidewalk.

The front door was open, and he could hear the voices of the emergency personnel, the click squawks of their mics and their clipped measured tones, speaking over the sound of a hysterically crying baby.

He practically ran through the front door then froze at the sight of a woman strapped onto a stretcher. All he could see was curly hair, stained and matted with blood, hanging off the edge.

The house had the living room in the front and the kitchen in the back with a long flight of stairs in between leading up to the bedrooms.

More blood was streaked along the stairway wall and pooled at the foot of the steps.

Swallowing the bile rising in his throat as his chest filled with terror and dread, he took a step toward the stretcher as he called out her name. "Leni!"

Relief flooded through him as she stepped out of the kitchen, bouncing the crying baby on her chest. Her eyes were wide as she tried to focus on the stretcher, reaching one hand out to the prone figure who must be her sister, while using the other to try to calm the distraught child.

She had on a pair of black shorts and a sleeveless top, and red blood was streaked along one of her hands and up her arm. Another dab of blood was smudged across her forehead.

He strode toward Leni, sweeping her and the baby into his arms, careful not to crush them, but needing to hold her. "I got you," he said into Leni's hair.

Her free arm wrapped around his back, her fingers gripping his shirt as she pressed into his chest. She whispered his name before pulling away, her eyes big and scared as she stared up at him, words tumbling out of her mouth over the cries of the baby. "Lorna. She fell down the stairs. Hit her head. I heard her fall. So much blood. I didn't know what to do. She passed out when she tried to stand up, so I called the ambulance."

"You did the right thing," he told her, gently taking the baby from her and rubbing the infant's back as he tucked her into the spot between his chest and his neck. She was so tiny. He could almost cover her whole body with his palm.

He pulled Leni back into the crook of his shoulder, holding her tightly against him as he offered soft coos and shushes against the downy soft hair of the baby's head.

Chevy heard another cry and turned to see Max, who had been curled into a small ball in the corner of the sofa, crawl down and launch himself toward them. He squeezed between them, clinging to both Chevy and Leni's legs.

Leni reached down and cupped his head. "It's okay, honey."

One of the paramedics—a tall black man with a

reassuring smile—walked toward them as the other one maneuvered the stretcher out the front door and toward the waiting ambulance. "I'm sure your sister's going to be fine," he told Leni. "Her ankle is pretty swollen, and she's probably gonna need a few stitches where she cut her head. We're taking her to the hospital where they'll assess her injuries, run a few tests, probably get an x-ray of her leg. You're welcome to follow us so you can be with her at the hospital, but we're leaving now."

"I don't know what to do," Leni cried as she looked up at Chevy. "I don't even have my car here. It's plugged in at the library. And I can't leave the kids. But I don't want Lorna to be by herself."

He put his keys into her hand. "Take my truck. I'll stay here with the kids."

"No. I can't ask you to do that. I'll call…" She pressed her hand to her mouth. "I don't know who to call."

"You don't have to call anyone. I've got this." He cupped her chin in his palm, tilting her face up toward his as he spoke in a low, calm tone. "She's going to be okay. I can handle the kids. You follow the ambulance in my truck and call me when you know something. I'm only a phone call or a text away. My number's the same. Do you need me to give it to you again?" He'd never changed it, just in case she ever decided to reach out to him.

"No, I've still got it." She clasped his keys to her chest as she pressed her lips together, so hard that he knew she was doing everything she could to hold it together.

He shrugged out of his flannel shirt, gently shifting Izzy—who had calmed down and stopped crying as she snuggled into the warmth of his shoulder—and held it out to Leni. "Put this on."

She must have been in shock because she didn't argue with him. She just pulled the shirt on. The sleeves were too long, but she didn't seem to notice as she wrapped the rest of the shirt around her body.

Her eyes still looked glazed, so he gripped one of her shoulders, just hard enough to get her to look up at him. "Listen to me, Eleanor Gibbs you can *do* this. For Pete's sake, you told me that you help build spacecraft for a living. Now you're going to get in my truck, drive to the hospital, and take care of your little sister. Because she needs you."

She stared into his eyes as if drawing strength from his gaze, then she nodded and pressed a kiss to Izzy's head before bending down to pull Max into a hug. His small arms wrapped around her neck, stretching the sleeves of his Paw Patrol pajamas as he hugged her tight. "Aunt Leni, is my mommy gonna be okay?"

Leni squeezed him to her, forcing a smile as she used the back of her hand to swipe away the tears from her cheeks. "Yes, of course she is, buddy. I know this seems scary, but those people who were here are taking good care of your mommy. And I'm going to the hospital to keep an eye on her. Are you okay staying with Chevy?"

He nodded, reaching to take Chevy's hand. "Yes. I want you to go. I don't want mommy to be all alone in the big hospital."

"Oh, sweet boy." She pressed a kiss to his cheek. "She won't be. I'll be with her the whole time."

The front door was still open, and Chevy could see the ambulance pulling away. "Better go," he told Leni.

She hurried to the door and stuffed her feet into a pair of sneakers that had been left there. Gripping the door frame, she turned back to Chevy. "You sure?"

He nodded, giving her his most sincere expression. "Yes. I got this. Go."

"Lorna just fed Izzy so she should be okay for a few hours. Call if you need me."

"Go."

"Thank you," she mouthed before turning and running across the lawn and toward his truck.

He closed the door behind her then scooped Max up into his arms. "Don't worry, bud. Your mom is gonna be fine. And I know she wouldn't want you to worry. How about we get you a drink of water then I'll read you a book before you go back to bed."

Max wrinkled his nose as he pondered the idea then held up two fingers. "Two books?"

Chevy squinted at him as if he were considering the negotiation. "Okay. *Three* books. But that's my final offer."

Max giggled. "Deal."

The memories washed over her as Leni climbed into Chevy's truck. It wasn't the same one they used to ride around in together—this one was newer—but it still smelled the same. Like him. A heady mixture of warm leather, sunbaked dirt, a hint of horse blanket, and the woodsy scent of his cologne.

A shiver ran through her, and she wrapped the sides of his shirt around her. The flannel smelled like him too and only fueled more memories.

Shoving the memories down, she reached to start the truck and noticed the rust-colored blood dried across her wrist and up her arm. Stifling a cry, she scrubbed at the blood with the sleeve of Chevy's shirt. She knew what he did on the ranch and was sure this faded flannel had seen worse than a spatter of dried blood.

Pull it together, girl.

She sat up in the seat, pushed her shoulders back and inhaled a deep breath. She had no idea why the hell Chevy Lassiter had walked into their house at the exact moment that she needed him, but he was right about one thing. Lorna needed her now.

And she *could* do this.

She put the truck in drive and then spent the whole ten-minute drive repeating the phrase, "Please God, let Lorna be okay."

Leni might be the big sister, but she counted on Lorna for so many things. And her kids needed their mommy. She had to be okay.

It was just after midnight when they finally released Lorna. They'd been there over four hours, and she'd gotten five stitches in her head and an ex-ray that showed a fracture in her ankle. After wrapping it, the doctor let her go with instructions to come back in a few days after the swelling had gone down and they'd determine if she needed a cast or if she'd be able to get by with just a walking boot.

Not that she was going to be doing much walking. The doctor had also given her a set of crutches and strict orders to keep her leg elevated and to ice it every few hours for the next few days.

A nurse helped Lorna into a wheelchair while Leni ran out to get the truck and met them at the front door. Together, she and the nurse got her sister up into the truck, and Leni carefully buckled her in then tucked the bag with all the instructions and medications behind the seat.

"Did you steal this truck?" her sister asked as Leni climbed into the driver's seat and started the engine. "Because I'm not sure they'll let me breastfeed in jail, and my boobs are killing me." She wrapped her arm across her swollen chest then leaned her head back against the seat and closed her eyes. "Actually, my whole body is killing me."

"You took quite a fall. You'll probably have bruises popping up all over the next few days," Leni said, avoiding the comment about the truck.

They both knew who the pickup belonged to.

"I hate these crutches already," Lorna said, ten minutes later as Leni tried to help her up the steps to the house. The railing had long since rotted and fallen off, which made the steps even more treacherous and hard to maneuver. "How am I going to carry the baby using these?"

Leni heard the catch in her sister's voice. Lorna hadn't cried yet, but she could tell she was on the verge. The stupid crutches might be what pushed her over the edge.

"I'll help you," Leni said, wrapping her arm around Lorna's waist as they managed another step. "Whatever you need."

They were both out of breath as they made it through the front door, then Lorna stopped, her mouth falling open as she peered around the room. "What the hell happened to my house?"

Chapter Seven

Leni stood next to her sister and gaped at the transformation of the house. The toys that had been strewn across the floor were neatly corralled in a bin, and the two loads of laundry that Lorna had dumped in the chair three days ago and had been meaning to get to, were all neatly folded and stacked in the laundry basket. The end tables had been straightened, and the carpet showed fresh vacuum tracks.

The kitchen had been cleaned as well. The supper dishes that Lorna had been coming down the stairs to do when she'd tripped on a Lego and fallen, were either in the dishwasher or drying in the rack next to an immaculately scrubbed sink. The floor had been freshly swept and mopped. Even the sticky fingerprints that Leni had noticed on the refrigerator earlier that day were gone.

The table and countertops had been wiped clean, and a candle that had been buried behind a stack of papers for weeks was now lit and sitting in the center of the counter, giving off a soft glow and the subtle scent of vanilla.

Lorna's eyes were still wide as she gazed around the house in awe. "Who did all this?" she whispered. As if talking too loudly might make the magical transformation disappear.

"I'm not sure," Leni said. "I guess Chevy must have."

"Dang, his grandma raised him right," Lorna said. "Do you think we could hire him to come do this every week?"

Leni laughed but what her sister said wasn't a bad idea, and she made a mental note to check into finding a cleaning service she could hire for the next four to six weeks.

As they started the slow and arduous task of getting Lorna up the stairs, Leni was thankful that Chevy, or the magical housecleaning fairies, had cleaned the blood off the wall and removed the stained rug from in front of the stairs. She made another mental note to order a new one from Amazon.

They stopped to check on Max as they passed his room, both leaning in and sighing together as they saw him tucked into bed and heard his soft snores filling the room.

They passed Leni's room next, which doubled as the nursery, and they could see Chevy asleep in the chair by the window, still holding Izzy on his chest. His cowboy hat was on the dresser and his boots were next to the chair.

"I'd like to let them sleep," Lorna said in a hushed voice. "But I'm sure Izzy is going to need to eat soon, and I'd rather feed her before I fall asleep."

"Good idea. Let's get you into bed then I'll bring her to you," Leni whispered back.

"I can help," Chevy said quietly, his eyes fluttering open. He eased up from the chair, the baby still cradled against his shoulder. "You should have woken me. I would have carried you up the stairs."

"Be still my beating heart," Lorna whispered to Leni. "If I weren't in so much pain, I might have just swooned."

"Oh, stop it," Leni whispered back as she started to nudge her sister in the ribs, then stopped herself.

The hallway was suddenly very crowded as the tall, broad cowboy stepped into it with them.

"I can pass Izzy to you," he told Leni. "But I don't want to wake her up."

"It's okay," Lorna told him. "I need to feed her anyway."

Leni took the baby from him, much calmer than she'd been earlier in the evening, but Izzy still stirred, her tiny mouth already making sucking motions as she rooted and fussed against Leni's shoulder.

Chevy took the crutches from Lorna, leaned them against the wall, then bent down and carefully scooped her into his arms. Watchful not to whack her head or her injured foot into the wall, he carried her into her room at the end of the hall and gently set her on the bed. "You need anything?"

"There's an ice pack in the freezer and a bag from the hospital on the sofa downstairs," Leni told him. "It's got some acetaminophen in it. Could you grab those and maybe a glass of water? There's a pink Stanley cup on the counter. Or there was."

"I saw it. It's in the dish strainer," Chevy said.

"Thanks for cleaning everything up," Lorna told

him, wincing as she tried to lean back against the pillow.

"Yeah, thanks." Leni shifted the pillow in an effort to make her sister more comfortable. "I can't believe you did all that."

He shrugged off their thanks. "The kids were asleep, and I wanted to do something to help. I live in a house with all men, so believe me, a sink full of dishes and a few baskets of laundry was nothing."

Leni put a hand on his arm and looked up at him, trying to ignore the heat she felt just from touching his skin. "No. It was *everything*. You really came through for me…for us…tonight."

"I would do anything for you." He held her gaze for a moment, as if trying to communicate his sincerity through this one look. And the weird thing was that she felt it. She'd grown up with this man, known him since she was twelve years old, and been in love with him since she was fourteen. A few days ago, he'd asked her if she was going to be staying in town long enough for him to try to get her to forgive him, and the idea of that seemed crazy.

How could she ever forgive him for the way he'd hurt her?

But maybe her sister was right.

Maybe he *had* changed.

Izzy took that moment to let out a frustrated cry, breaking their gaze as Leni passed the baby to her sister.

"Leni texted me a few hours ago with instructions on how to give her a bottle," Chevy said. "But I only gave her a couple of ounces of milk—just enough to stave her off—because I figured you'd need to nurse her when you got home."

"Thanks for that," Lorna told him.

"I'll go get that water and the medicine," Chevy said, ducking out of the room as Lorna settled the baby in next to her.

Leni heard his footsteps on the stairs as she turned back to her sister. "What else can I do for you? Do you want another pillow?"

Lorna winced as Izzy latched on, then her shoulders relaxed. "I'm good now. But Chevy really came through tonight, didn't he?"

"Yeah, he did. Although I still have no idea where he even came from. It was crazy. You were bleeding, the ambulance was there, Izzy was crying. Everything was happening at once, then he was just *there*."

"Sometimes it happens like that," Lorna said, running her fingers over the pale blond peach fuzz on Izzy's small head. "Everything happens at once, then they just show up, right where they're supposed to be. And then everything just feels right."

"I've got her stuff," Chevy said, coming up the stairs. "Do you want to come get it?"

"Aww. Isn't he thoughtful?" Lorna tried to waggle her eyebrows, but grimaced as the movement must have caused pain around her stitches.

Leni walked into the hallway to meet Chevy. He was holding the bag with the Tylenol, a Spiderman ice pack, and two Stanley cups of water.

"This was the only ice pack I saw. And I figured you could use some water too," he told Leni as he handed her all the things. "You probably haven't had anything to drink since this all happened."

Dang it. Lorna was right. He *was* thoughtful.

"No, I haven't. Thank you." She took a sip from the straw and the cool water felt amazing on her throat. "How'd you get so good with babies?"

"I've grown up on a ranch and bottle-fed just about every kind of baby farm animal there is—from calves to colts to newborn kittens."

"Are you comparing my adorable niece to a baby cow?" Leni teased him.

He held his hands up in surrender. "No, I wouldn't dare."

"She is as cute as a kitten, but the way you just scooped Izzy up and didn't seem intimidated at all by holding her or giving her a bottle, that's something different." A thought occurred to her, and it felt as if the blood suddenly drained from her face. "Do you have a kid? Or a wife?" Surely Lorna would have told her if Chevy had gotten married.

Chevy chuckled. "No. And absolutely not. Not married and no kids. But there have been several moms who've brought their newborns to knitting club, and I became the designated baby-holder."

Relief flooded through, but her cheeks still felt tingly at the memory of Chevy holding her niece so comfortably in the crook of his shoulder. "Is that how you knew Lorna would want to nurse? That was kind of impressive, by the way."

"Thanks. And yes. Knitting Club could also be called Chatting Club, because all those women do is talk. And the older women love giving advice to the younger ones, especially the new moms. I've heard more than I ever wanted to know about mastitis, leaking milk, and bleeding nipples."

Leni's eyes widened as she crossed her arms over her chest. "*Bleeding* nipples?"

He shrugged. "Evidently cracks are a thing unless you use cream after. But, apparently Bag Balm, the stuff they use on cow's utters, works great."

"Weird, but I'll let my sister know." She held up the things in her hands. "Let me give this stuff to Lorna and get her settled, then I'll come back to talk to you."

He nodded. "My boots are in your room. Okay if I wait for you in there?"

"Yes, that's fine." She turned away, the thought of him being in her room again after all these years making her heart race.

It took her longer than she'd thought it would to take care of her sister. By the time she'd found pillows to elevate Lorna's leg, positioned the ice pack carefully on her ankle, gave her the Tylenol and set up her night table with her water, the extra pain reliever, a tube of chap stick, and got her phone plugged into the charger, Izzy had finished nursing and fallen asleep. Lorna was practically asleep herself as Leni took the baby and gently placed her in the bassinet next to the bed.

"Call me if you need anything," Leni whispered before slipping out of the room. Taking a deep breath, she walked back to her room, not sure what she was going to say to Chevy but knowing that she needed to really thank him for all he'd done for her family that night.

She rounded her door frame then stopped, her heart stuck in her throat, as she took in the sight of Chevy Lassiter curled up on one side of her bed, sound asleep with his head on the pillow next to hers.

Chapter Eight

LENI LET CHEVY sleep as she took a quick shower then brushed her teeth and changed into a fresh tank top and clean pajama shorts. It was the least she could do. He had to be exhausted. She was too, but she needed to wash the smell of blood and the emergency room off her.

His snores, louder than the cute ones they'd listened to Max making earlier, filled the room as she tiptoed back in and sat on the edge of the bed. She could go downstairs to sleep on the couch and let him have her room, but she wanted to be near Lorna and Max, in case they needed something in the night.

Her shoulders fell. Plus, she was too dang tired to even walk down the stairs. She laid her head on the pillow, curling on her side with her back to Chevy, careful to stay on her side of the bed.

As she lay there, trying to relax her body, the events of the night finally caught up to her—all the fear of finding her sister at the bottom of the stairs, the blood around her head, and the terror of trying to grab her as Lorna passed out and fell again.

It was all too much, and the emotions hit her all at

once. A sob bubbled up in her throat, and she pressed her fist to her mouth. Her shoulders shook as tears stung her eyes.

Then Chevy's arm was around her, pulling her back to spoon against him. His lips were against her ear, his voice low and comforting as he told her, "It's okay, darlin'. You can cry now."

He knew her so well—knew the way she held it all together during a crisis then broke down once it was all over and everything was okay.

Her brain reminded her that she was supposed to be angry with him, but her traitorous body didn't care. She rolled over, taking solace in his arms as she let him hold her while the floodgates released, and she sobbed against his chest.

"It's okay." He stroked his hand over her head as he whispered into her hair. "Let it all out. Lorna's gonna be okay. Everybody's okay."

When her tears finally ran out, she pulled back and peered up at him. "Sorry about that."

"Stop. You don't ever have to be sorry for showing emotion or for leaning on me."

Leaning on him? She bristled, her shoulders tightening. She hadn't been able to lean on him for a very long time.

He must have felt the change in her body, because he kept his tone low and even. "It was a lot tonight, but you did great."

She huffed out a laugh. "No. I didn't. I completely fell apart. I see myself as a smart, capable woman. I can write software code and can literally get lost for hours calculating the eigenvector slew of a spacecraft, but when my sister was bleeding and passed out in my arms, I was at a complete loss. Izzy was crying and Max was terrified, and I just stood there."

"First of all, you were in shock. Nobody thinks straight when they're in shock. Second of all, what the hell is an eigenvector slew?"

She laughed, and the tightness of her body released with the shift. "It's the method of calculating a steering correction, called a slew, by rotating a spacecraft around one fixed axis." She shook her head. "It doesn't matter. The thing I'm trying to say is that *you* were the real hero. I have no idea why or how you showed up when you did, but you saved the day."

"I'm glad I could help. I meant it when I said I would do anything for you."

Anything but stay in love with me.

The thought brought back the anger, but she was too exhausted to hold onto it. Chevy really had done so much. And maybe it was that she was too beat to care or maybe there was a part of her—a part she didn't want to think too much about—who was happy to be back in Chevy's arms, happy to have him holding her and telling her everything was going to be okay.

Their bodies had changed, his shoulders were broader, and she was quite a bit curvier than she'd been at eighteen, but they still fit perfectly together. Her mind could deny it, but her body knew. She'd slid into place next to him as easily as that final piece fits into an assembled puzzle—with a smooth click and a small sigh that signaled a feeling of completeness.

Leni had been leaving a night light on in her room, in case Lorna needed anything for the baby or Max needed her. The soft glow of the small light was enough to see Chevy's face in the otherwise dark room, and now he was holding not just her body, but her gaze as he stared into her eyes, as if trying to communicate ten years' worth of emotion and discussion without actually saying a word.

Except she *needed* to hear his words, needed to understand what had happened, why he had changed, why he had been so in love with her and dreaming of a future together then suddenly claiming he didn't love her at all.

But not tonight.

Neither her brain—nor her heart—would be able to handle that kind of conversation after the night she'd just had.

No—for now, she was content to lay in the circle of his arms, to appreciate the kind and thoughtful ways he'd taken care of her and her family—and to let him hold her.

She didn't have to say any of that either. She was sure he knew. Mainly because she was looking back at him with true affection versus the murderous rage she was sure she'd had in her eyes that first day she'd seen him in the Mountain Brew and had been contemplating killing him and grinding his body up in the coffee bean grinder.

His gaze held affection as well. Then it dropped to her lips and changed into something else. Something like hunger and heat. And *need*.

She tried to take in a breath, but it caught in her throat as her heart suddenly felt like it was beating a million miles per hour.

While he looked at her lips, she studied his face.

She knew it so well, knew the shape of his blue eyes, and the curve of his lips, although he hadn't had the scruff of dark beard in his teens that he had now.

She reached up to touch the tiny scar at the edge of his eyebrow, remembering how he'd cut it diving into the lake one hot summer day when they'd snuck up to go swimming at his family's hunting cabin that was tucked into the mountains above the ranch.

That day had been perfect. If she closed her eyes, she could almost feel the warm sun on her skin and smell the algae in the clear blue water of the mountain lake.

Chevy had snuck out some food from the kitchen at the ranch, and she remembered eating greasy potato chips and cold fried chicken—his grandma June's famous recipe—and drinking iced tea from Mason jars as they sunned themselves on a giant boulder at the edge of the water. They'd kissed and made out, and she could remember the feel of the rough warm rock against her bare back and how brazen she'd felt when Chevy had loosened the ties of her bikini top and tossed it onto the bank.

He'd looked down at her half-naked body then about the same way he was looking at her mouth now. Heat coiled in her belly, and she tingled in places that hadn't felt tingly in a long time.

She knew she shouldn't—knew she would regret the action—but she couldn't help herself. Her touch was feathery light, barely grazing his skin as she reached up and ran her finger across the scar. But it was enough for Chevy's eyes to flutter closed and for him to suck in a breath as his hold on her waist tightened.

His eyes opened, but they narrowed as he shifted

closer, and his arm brushed the side of her breast. Her nipples tightened as his gaze dipped to her chest, the pebbled nubs pushing through the light fabric of her pajama top, and they were both now very aware that she wasn't wearing a bra.

Chapter Nine

Chevy leaned closer still, close enough that Leni could smell his cologne and feel the warmth of his breath on her cheek.

She held perfectly still, frozen like a rabbit caught in the sight of a wolf, on one hand terrified of what would happen next, on the other praying that the wolf would capture and devour her.

Oh.

Inhaling a shaky breath, her fingers still resting on his forehead, she let them roam softly around his eye, over his cheekbone, and then down to brush lightly along his lower lip.

His lips parted, and she continued her exploration, thrilling at his sharp catch of breath as her thumb grazed the edge of his mouth.

It was his turn to hold stock still, and he didn't move as she skimmed her fingers along his cheek, over the scruff of beard then slid them into the thick locks of his hair.

His hand was still at her waist. He slid it along her back, his long fingers kneading her skin as he pulled her closer still.

He dipped his head, his lips just brushing against hers, and the small tingling she'd felt before, now changed to flames of heat, racing through her veins.

Her fingers dug further into his hair, gripping his head as his lips—finally—pressed to hers, taking her mouth in the kind of kiss she'd only let herself dream about in the small quiet hours of the rare nights she'd allowed herself to think about him.

His mouth was warm, the kiss urgent as he pulled her closer. Then her arms were around his neck, and she was pressing her body into him, kissing him back with all a fervor she didn't know was even in her.

She wanted him. It didn't matter that it had been ten years since they'd seen each other. Here, in the darkness of her old bedroom, all she cared about was Chevy Lassiter's mouth and having his hands on her body.

As if he read her mind, his hand slipped beneath the back of her shirt and his fingers skimmed over her skin. Up her back, along her side, the edge of his fingers grazing the side of her boob. She moaned against his lips as his hand slid between them and his palm cupped her breast, swollen and aching with need. His thumb slid over the pebble of her tightened nipple, sending a shot of heat to her core.

She pressed her hips into his, grinding against the hard swell of his erection.

She was in trouble here.

If Chevy Lassiter chose to rip her clothes off and take her right now, she would be powerless to stop him.

His fingers skimmed just inside the elastic waist of her pajama shorts, and she wrapped her leg around his, her body eager and willing, even as her mind tried to stay rational.

She held her breath, anticipating his touch.

His hand dipped inside her shorts.

Ohhhh.

This was happening. Nothing could stop it.

A heart-wrenching cry broke the silence of the house as Isabel declared she was either hungry or in distress over a wet diaper.

Leni fell back against the mattress, her breath coming in hard pants.

Apparently, the ill-timed distress call from her sweet baby niece *could* stop the barreling train of desire.

"I'll be right back," she whispered as she got out of bed then adjusted her pajamas as she hurried toward Lorna's room to help.

But she wasn't right back.

It took her and her sister longer than she'd anticipated to get Izzy quieted and settled into a spot that didn't cause discomfort for Lorna's ankle. Middle of the night feedings didn't typically take long, but Lorna could barely keep her eyes open, so Leni just waited for Izzy to finish, then carefully took the baby from her sister and tucked her back into the bassinet.

Taking a deep breath, she walked back down the hall to her bedroom, not sure what to expect. The moment had been broken. Which was maybe okay because things had gotten pretty intense really quickly.

She was met with the sounds of Chevy's even breathing as she tiptoed back into the room. Apparently, she'd been gone longer than she thought.

Slipping under the sheets, she snuggled her back up against his chest, spooning her body into his. She wasn't sure if he completely woke up or was still half-asleep as he wrapped his arm around her, the motion feeling almost protective as he pulled her close and pressed his cheek to the side of her head.

Then his breathing evened out again, and she closed her eyes and relaxed into him.

Just for tonight.

The next morning, something stirred Leni awake, and she found herself staring into a pair of beautiful blue eyes.

Not the eyes she'd been dreaming about though. Those belonged to a man.

The ones she was staring into did belong to a *little* man though. One who was standing next to her bed and scratching a bug bite on the side of his arm.

"Hey Max," she said, stifling a yawn as she pushed up onto her elbow. Sunlight streamed through her window, and her bedside clock read close to eight. She was surprised he'd let her sleep for so long. He was normally up before seven. Although the night before had been anything but normal. "You okay?"

He nodded. He'd already changed out of his pajamas and into a pair of shorts and a yellow T-shirt with a one-eyed minion on the front.

"How long have you been standing there?" she asked, suddenly remembering that she wasn't alone in her bed.

He lifted his shoulders then let them drop again.

"I don't know. I can't tell time yet. Maybe for about twenty snores though."

She laughed. "I do *not* snore." But maybe the cowboy in the bed behind her did. "Is there something I can do for you?"

He shifted from one small foot to the other. "I checked on Mommy and Izzy, and they're both asleep. Last night was scary, and I wanted to do something nice for Mommy so I thought I could make her some breakfast. But I don't really know how to make anything. Except frozen waffles. And Mommy doesn't like me to use the toaster by myself."

Her heart melted.

"That's really nice of you, buddy. She would love that. And I'm happy to help you. Just give me a few minutes to get up and dressed." And have what she was sure would be a super awkward moment when Chevy woke up next to her. "Can you go down to the kitchen and wait for me?"

His little face broke into a grin, and he bobbed his head up and down in an excited nod. "Thanks Aunt Leni."

As Max left her room, she rolled over to nudge Chevy awake.

But the other side of her bed was empty.

Chapter Ten

Her heart in her throat, Leni sat up and looked around her bedroom. Chevy's blue and white flannel shirt was still draped across the arm of her chair, but his cowboy boots and hat were gone.

Flinging the sheets aside, she pushed out of bed and hurried to the window. His truck was gone too.

Wow.

Last night, he'd been so caring and attentive. And *that kiss.*

She'd fallen asleep with her back spooned against his chest and his warm breath caressing her neck.

But now he'd left without even saying goodbye? She glanced around the room, hoping maybe he'd left a note.

Nope. No note. No goodbye.

No cowboy.

What a jerk. An ache tightened her chest as she tried to tell herself that it didn't matter. She'd been good without him for the last decade—*well, maybe not good, but just fine*—so she sure as hell didn't need him now.

But dang, it sure had been nice to step into the past and feel like she was his again. Just for a little while.

It took her longer than she'd meant to get dressed and brush her teeth and hair. Mainly because she kept getting distracted by thoughts of a certain cowboy who had apparently snuck out sometime in the night or early morning. She must have been really zonked out since she hadn't heard him leave.

She peeked in on her sister and winced at the matted rust-colored blood dried in Lorna's blond hair, but glad that Izzy was letting her sleep. The door creaked as she started to pull it closed.

Lorna stirred and lifted her hand in a small wave as she whispered, "It's okay. I'm awake. Barely." She lifted her head off the pillow. "Is Max up?"

"Yes. He wants to make you breakfast," Leni whispered back. "So, get some more rest before Izzy wakes up. I've got it covered."

She gently pulled the door closed, hoping her sister could sleep for a bit longer and then tiptoed down the stairs. She stepped into the living room to see Max kneeling against the back of the sofa and staring intently at something out the window.

"What are you looking at, buddy?" she asked, as she crossed the room. Wildlife was abundant in their neighborhood, especially since their house was so close to the creek, and she assumed her nephew was watching a deer or a bunny in the yard.

"I'm just watching all the people," he told her as he pointed out the window. "Are we having a party?"

"Not that I'm aware of," she said, coming up behind him. Her eyes widened at the cars and trucks that were pulling up in front of their house.

Including Chevy's pickup.

She hurried to the front door and pulled it open. What the heck were all these people doing here?

Max followed her out onto the porch and waved excitedly to Chevy, who was unloading a stack of two by fours from the back of his truck. Another pickup had pulled up behind his, with Chevy's brother, Dodge, and Maisie, the librarian he was seeing, inside.

Duke Lassiter and a tall curvy blond woman she'd never seen before got out of another car and walked across the lawn toward her.

"What are you all doing here?" she asked into Duke's shoulder as he engulfed her in a big cookie-scented bear hug.

She'd never really known her grandparents, and Duke was the closest thing she'd ever had to a grandpa. Losing Chevy had been heart-achingly awful, but she'd also mourned the loss of the Lassiter family in her life. She let herself be held by him for just a moment. Why did this man always smell like fresh laundry and vanilla?

"Chevy came into the ranch house this morning loaded for bear, and he rallied the troops. He told us what happened to Lorna, and we're all here to help," Duke told her, giving her one more squeeze before letting her go. "It's awful good to see you, Leni. We've missed you, darlin'."

She swallowed back the emotion filling her throat. "Good to see you, too."

"Hi, I'm Ford's girlfriend, Elizabeth," the woman with Duke said, holding up a box filled with orange juice, a couple of plastic containers, and a red casserole dish covered in foil. The smile on her face was warm and kind, like they were already friends. "We brought breakfast."

Max grinned up at Leni. "I was just wishing that we already *had* breakfast and didn't have to make it."

She had spent the better part of the last twenty minutes wishing that Chevy hadn't just snuck out in the middle of the night and that she would hear from him again today.

Apparently, both her *and* Max's wishes had come true.

"Wow. You didn't have to do this," Leni tried to tell them, but Max already had the front door open and was pointing the way to the kitchen.

"We know," Duke said with a wink as he walked past her. "But we wanted to."

Dodge's girlfriend came up the stairs, holding a blue grocery tote. Leni remembered her a little from school, and they had met again a few weeks ago when she and Dodge had come into the coffee shop. "I'm not sure if you remember me. I'm Maisie. I was in Lorna's class, and I work at the library."

Leni nodded. "Yes, of course, I do. You're with Dodge, right?"

The other woman's cheeks blushed pink, which Leni thought was kind of adorable. She didn't know Maisie well, but she seemed very nice.

"Well, yes, I guess." She held up the tote bag. "My grandma is Ruby Foster, I think you know her too, and she sent me with a baked ziti she had in the freezer, and I brought taco meat and all the fixings for you all. Some of the other women from the church will probably be dropping meals off later today or tomorrow. We didn't want you or Lorna to have to cook."

"Gosh, this is so nice. I don't know what to say."

Maisie smiled. "Just say thanks and then bring a meal to someone in town next time you hear they're in need."

"Thank you." She could handle the 'thanks' part, but she wasn't planning to be in town long enough to help the next person in need.

Although…her stomach dropped as she suddenly realized that she wasn't going to be able to leave in a week or so, like she'd originally planned. Not with her sister hobbling around on crutches for the next six weeks. Lorna had done so much for her over the years and never asked for anything in return.

There was no way Leni was leaving, not when her sister needed her, and she could actually do something to help.

There was only one complication with her staying for longer, and he was wearing a sexy-as-sin grin as he walked across the lawn toward her.

"Good mornin', darlin'," he said, as he dropped a stack of boards and a pile of tools next to the porch. He lowered his voice to a whisper. "Sorry I didn't say goodbye this morning. I was up early, and you were sleeping so soundly, I didn't want to wake you. I was hoping to get my chores taken care of and get back before you woke up. And I figured getting home to Duke and the ranch was the best place to start to round you all up some help."

She didn't know what to say. She was still stuck on the way her stomach had done a little belly flop when he'd called her 'darlin'. And she appreciated the way he whispered and wasn't announcing to the whole town of Woodland Hills that he'd spent the night with her.

Although his truck had been parked in front of their house, so word had probably already spread.

"What is all that for?" she asked as Dodge walked up with a circular saw and another handful of boards.

"Hey Leni," Dodge said, his shit-eatin' grin telling her he already knew where his brother had spent the night.

Chevy gestured to the stairs leading up to the front porch. "Those steps are treacherous enough as it is without trying to manage them in crutches like Lorna's going to be doing, so I thought Dodge and I could build her a couple of railings. One for each side."

"Um…wow…that would be a really nice surprise for her." Had she mentioned the night before the trouble they'd had trying to navigate the stairs with Lorna's broken ankle? Or had Chevy just noticed the need and come up with a solution?

"That's not the only surprise I have for her," he said, grinning like a kid who had just been given the new toy they'd been wanting.

Leni stared at him as he backtracked to the truck and pulled a blue knee-scooter from the bed.

He carried it back across the yard and set it down in front of her like it was a prize he was awarding. "Check this out. It's going to make her life so much easier than trying to manage a set of crutches."

"Where in the world did you get a knee-scooter already this morning?" she asked, not able to keep the incredulity out of her voice.

"One of the gals in the knitting club had one from when she got a knee replacement last year," he explained. "You have to give it back, but she was happy to loan it to Lorna to use. It even has a basket." He tapped the pink and white basket attached to the front of the scooter. "Her name is Betty."

She raised an eyebrow. "The knee-scooter has a name?"

"Oh yeah. Betty the Balance Buddy. And from what I hear, she'd got a personality too. But if you're good to her, she'll be good to you."

Leni let out a laugh. "I'll let Lorna know." Then her mouth went dry as he slung a tool belt around his lean hips and dropped a hammer into the ring on its side.

What was it about a man in a tool belt?

Holy hot handy cowboy.

Dodge had already pulled out a tape measure and was marking up two by fours with a pencil and a framing square. He looked up at her with a sheepish grin. "Guess we owe you an apology for the coffee gag we pulled on you and Chev. We just thought it would be a funny way for Chevy to find out you were still in town. We didn't mean any harm. Sorry if we upset you."

She sighed. "No harm done. And in retrospect, it was kind of funny to have Chevy rolling up to the counter and trying to order a…what was it…a purple unicorn volcano."

Dodge laughed. "That one was mine."

"Yeah, you guys were hilarious," Chevy told him, with a playful shove to the shoulder.

Leni laughed along with them. It felt good to be

around the guys she'd practically grown up with again.

Dodge held a board up to the side of the steps, marked it, then tucked the pencil behind his ear. He wore a baseball cap over his blond hair instead of a cowboy hat, and she could still see the boy she remembered—the one who used to find a shady spot on the farm and read for hours—in his features. It made perfect sense that a total bookworm like him would end up with a librarian.

She'd only seen him and Maisie together a few times, but they seemed totally in love and like a really great fit for each other. Lorna told her that Maisie had been in love with Dodge since the tenth grade—and why wouldn't she be—the guy had always been sweet and was crazy good-looking.

All the Lassiter men were.

Including the one who kept sneaking glances at her and flashing her grins that made her pulse race like a car in the Daytona 500.

Stop looking at him.

Leni turned her attention back to the brother she didn't used to be in love with and was glad that Dodge had found someone who made him happy. But she wasn't so sure about the way he was fitting two of the boards together.

She eyed him skeptically. "Do you have any actual plans drawn up? Could I see the specs for these railings?"

Chevy laughed. "This isn't rocket science, Len. But don't worry. You know Duke's been teaching us how to properly build things since we were all ten years old."

"And we've all spent summers working in construction," Dodge added.

"We can manage two stair railings," Chevy assured her. "And I promise we'll do it right."

Her phone buzzed, saving her from offering any unwanted advice on their building skills, and she pulled it from her pocket to see her sister was calling.

"What is happening down there?" Lorna asked when she picked up.

"Apparently, Chevy called out the calvary, and the whole Lassiter clan, plus a few extras, showed up with food and offers to help. And he and Dodge are building you a set of railings for your front steps."

"You're kidding?"

"Nope. They've got boards and power tools and everything."

"Oh my gosh. That's so nice. I think I'm going to cry."

"Wait until you smell the breakfast stuff that Duke just carried into the kitchen."

"Are they all still here?"

"Oh yeah."

"I want to come down. Will you come up and help me with Izzy and these stupid crutches?"

"I'll be up in a minute." She hung up and pushed her phone back into the pocket of her shorts.

"Everything okay?" Chevy asked.

"Yes. This sweet stuff you all are doing is making Lorna cry. And she wants to see everyone, so I need to go up and help her get down the stairs."

"I can help too," he said, unclipping and dropping his tool belt to follow her into the house. "You can get Izzy, and I'll get your sister."

It took them a few minutes to change the baby, but Lorna had gotten out of bed and hobbled around enough to get herself dressed and to the bathroom to get her hair and teeth brushed.

At the top of the landing, Chevy scooped Lorna up again and carried her down the stairs, to the cheers and greetings of his family and their friends.

"Thank you everyone," she said, pressing a hand to her chest. "This is so nice."

"Wait until you meet Betty," Chevy told her with a sly grin.

She turned to Leni and mouthed, "Who's Betty?"

"You'll see," she mouthed back as Chevy set her sister down and ran outside.

Chevy came back in hauling the knee scooter and placed it in front of Lorna. "*This* is Betty."

Lorna was thrilled with the knee scooter and laughed as Max climbed up on the seat and tried to ride it around the living room. "This is really sweet. Thank you, Chevy."

He nodded. "It's no problem. I know what a pain crutches can be, and I was worried about how you were going to manage getting around with them." He eyed the knee-scooter. "We might even be able to rig the basket so you could set Izzy in it and not have to carry her while you're trying to maneuver this thing."

"Speaking of how you're going to get around. I was thinking we needed to bring the bassinet downstairs and pull out the sofa in the family room," Leni told her, referring to the living area at the back of the house behind the kitchen. "We can set it up for you to stay in there, at least for the first few weeks so you don't have to mess with the stairs. I'll still stay up there with Max, but we can construct a temporary changing station for Izzy and bring your toiletries down so you can use the main level bathroom."

Lorna smiled at her. "I love the way your brain is always coming up with a plan."

Chevy was grinning at her like a cat who'd just gobbled up a canary.

"What?" she asked, wondering if she had something in her teeth or had put her shirt on backwards.

He lifted his shoulders in a small shrug. "Nothin'. Except I think I just caught you telling your sister that you were going to be sticking around…at least for another few weeks."

Chapter Eleven

Leni was saved from answering Chevy by Duke calling them into the kitchen.

"Y'all come on in," Duke said. "Don't let this breakfast casserole get cold."

Chevy showed Lorna how to use the knee scooter, the way to position her injured leg on the cushioned pad and more importantly, how to use the handbrake, while Leni carried Izzy into the kitchen and placed her in the bouncy seat in the center of the table.

Maisie and Elizabeth cooed over the baby while Dodge set out the paper plates, plastic cups, and cutlery that Duke had brought. Chevy poured cups of milk and orange juice while Duke served up thick slices of an egg dish laden with country sausage, hash brown potatoes, and gooey cheddar cheese.

Elizabeth pulled herself away from playing with Izzy to set out a bowl of sliced berries then opened the last container, which was filled with mini muffins. The scents of bananas, nuts, and vanilla filled the air.

Leni took a muffin as the dish was passed around and popped it into her mouth. It was still warm, and she groaned at the delicious perfectly moist cake. "These are amazing," she told Elizabeth.

The other woman waved her compliment away. "They were easy. I whipped the batter up in five minutes. They took longer to bake than to make, and they were in the oven for less than fifteen minutes."

"You made these *this* morning?" she asked, in awe of Elizabeth. She'd barely gotten herself dressed and her teeth brushed.

"I'll give you the recipe," Elizabeth told her.

"Thanks."

Maisie raised her hand as if she were in a classroom. "Can I get it too?"

"Leni loves to bake," Chevy said. "Or I guess, you used to," he said after she'd shot him an arched eyebrow expression. "I remember you said baking was like chemistry, and you loved the preciseness of the measurements and the chemical reactions that the different ingredients combined to create. I always thought that was such a cool way to look at baking."

Leni blinked as heat warmed the back of her neck. She hadn't known he'd thought that. "I'm surprised you remembered such a funny thing about me."

"I remember everything," he told her, then cleared his throat as he must have realized everyone was staring at them. "And I could never forget your butterscotch and chocolate chip cookies. I still think about them."

I still think about you.

She tore her gaze from his. Not the time or the place to analyze that thought.

Turning back to Elizabeth, she tried to think of something to change the subject. "So, where's Ford this morning? Not that we need any *more* people squeezed into this kitchen, but I haven't seen him since I've been back in town."

"He stayed at the ranch to get the rest of the chores done," Elizabeth told her.

"You know, the oldest brother is always the most responsible one," Dodge said.

"And except for Elizabeth, Ford's usually happiest when he's on his own," Chevy explained. "You know how some people have FOMO, the fear of missing out. Ford more often has JOMO, the *joy* of missing out."

The group laughed together as Elizabeth nudged Chevy's shoulder. "Not that he would be joyful at missing out on seeing you, of course," she tried to tell Leni. "He's just more of a loner."

"And prefers the company of his dog to most people," Chevy added.

"I get it," Leni told Elizabeth. "I'm not offended. I've known these guys a long time." Although it had also *been* a long time since she'd seen or hung out with any of them. "And I'm thankful Ford took the bullet of the extra chores so Chevy and Dodge could build the railings for the stairs. They'll really help Lorna to get up and down those front steps."

"Not that I'm planning on going anywhere any time soon," Lorna said, gesturing to her bandaged ankle. Chevy had stacked a couple of throw pillows on the kitchen chair next to her and helped prop her foot up on them.

"Why would you need to?" Leni asked, grinning over at Maisie. "Now that we're set up with tacos and baked ziti. This seems like the perfect time to catch up on your reading or the latest season of Bridgerton."

Lorna let out a wistful sigh. "I *am* anxious to see what kind of mischief Lady Whistledown is up to. But I also miss my coffee shop. I haven't been there in weeks."

Leni glanced at the kitchen clock and popped out of her chair. "Oh shoot. Speaking of the coffee shop, we open in thirty minutes. I need to get ready to head down there."

No one came in before the church crowd, so they opened late on Sunday mornings and then were closed on Mondays.

"No, you don't," Elizabeth said. "Because we'd like to help you all with that, too."

"We would've just gone in and opened the store ourselves," Duke told her. "But we didn't have the keys to get in."

Elizabeth held a hand up to ward off Leni's objections. "Don't worry. I know my way around a coffee machine. I spent three summers in college working as a barista. Sometimes it felt like I was earning a degree in Caramel Macchiatos along with my Accounting one."

"And I can handle bussing the tables and serving pastries and generally chatting up the customers while Elizabeth makes the coffees," Duke told them. "I'm looking forward to it. It sounds like fun to me."

Leni exchanged looks with her sister. "I guess it would be okay. One of the Johnson girls, Emily, is scheduled to work today. She's still learning the drinks, but she's great at managing the register."

"It sounds great to me," Lorna said. "Experienced help that I don't have to put on the payroll and figure out taxes for? Yes, please. And honestly, I could really use my sister today." She turned to Elizabeth. "I know your family runs a restaurant, so I have every faith in your shop skills. And don't worry, within the first three days of taking over the place, Leni had re-organized my supply closet, created an opening and closing schedule, and made color-coded cards detailing exactly how to make all the drink recipes."

Leni looked down at her feet. "Sorry. It just made more sense to have it all organized and the recipes and closing procedures written down. And your supply room was total chaos—you had the plasticware next to the syrups and the coffee next to the cleaning supplies. Now it's all logical, and you can easily find things."

Lorna laughed. "Don't be sorry. I love having an engineer for a sister. And I know you can't help yourself when it comes to organizing and creating structure. So, I especially love it when my house and my store benefit from your giant brain."

"That settles it then," Duke said, putting what was left of the food into the refrigerator then wiping the last few stray crumbs from the counter into his palm and dumping them in the sink. "We'd better get going."

Leni wrote her and Lorna's numbers down then got the spare set of shop keys from the kitchen drawer and passed them all to Duke. "Emily should be there before ten, and she can show you how to get everything set up. And these are our numbers so don't hesitate to call or text us with any questions. And if you get stuck, or have a big rush, call me and I'll come down to help out."

"Don't you worry," he said, giving her a wink. "We've got this. You just take care of your family."

After Duke and Elizabeth left, Dodge took Max outside to help him work on the railings while Chevy carried the bassinet down to the back living room. Maisie helped Leni get the sofa bed made, and the room set up while Lorna nursed the baby.

"Ugh, I think there's still blood matted in my hair," Lorna said, as she nestled a sleeping Izzy into the bassinet.

"I can help you figure out how to cover your bandaged foot and forehead so you can take a shower before they put the cast on your ankle," Leni told her. "Then we can pack up some of your bathroom stuff and a few clothes to bring downstairs for you."

"I brought a book, so I'm happy to sit in here and watch the baby if that would help," Maisie offered.

"That would be great," Lorna told her.

It took almost an hour for Lorna to shower and for her and Leni to get everything moved down to the living room.

"I'm exhausted, and it's not even noon," Lorna said, leaning her head back so Leni could brush out her wet hair.

"I'd love to take Max down to the library to check out some books if you want to take a nap," Maisie said. "And if you have a stroller, I can take Izzy too."

"You're so sweet," Lorna told her. "The baby usually sleeps for a few hours in the morning, so I have another hour to nap, but I'm sure Max would love to go. He loves going to the library. But you've already done so much."

The librarian waved away her objection. "Nonsense. I'm happy to help. And I think this morning has been a ton of fun."

"First tacos and now taking Max on an adventure. I don't know how to repay you."

Maisie looked down at the sofa where she ran her finger over a broken seam. "You don't have to repay me anything, but I could always use another friend or two."

"Sold," Lorna and Leni said at the same time, then the three women laughed together.

Maisie collected her things while Lorna crashed out on the sofa.

"I'll walk you out," Leni told her, following her onto the front porch. Just to be polite. Nothing to do with wanting to check on the progress of the railings. Or the cute cowboy who was helping to build them.

Country music was playing from a speaker on their toolbox, and the two brothers were laughing with Max as Chevy held a board up to the frame they'd built along the side of the stairs while Dodge set a screw. They'd already made great progress. One of the railings looked to be finished.

Chevy held his hand out to steady Maisie as she maneuvered down the front steps and around the tools and boards.

"Oh, I love this one," Maisie said, as a new song started.

Still holding her hand, Chevy pulled her into his

arms and crooned loudly along with the lyrics as he two-stepped Maisie down the sidewalk. She stumbled as he spun her around in an intricate maneuver, then her face went pink as she let out a nervous giggle.

"Now, be careful with her," Dodge warned. "That's my girl you're tripping up there."

"Tripping is right," Maisie said with a laugh. "On my own two left feet. I can't do those complicated steps."

"You know who can?" Chevy asked as he passed Maisie off to Dodge then bounded up the steps to sweep Leni into his arms. "This girl right here. She's a great dancer." He triple-stepped her around the wide front porch then as the tempo of the chorus picked up, he swung her around, twisting their arms over and around their heads as he skillfully executed a pretzel.

It had been years since Leni had country danced. Heck, years since she'd danced at all, other than the few times by herself in the kitchen when a good song came on. But somehow, with Chevy, the boy who had taught her how to swing dance and two-step, she fell back into their old rhythm and all the steps came back to her as easy as shooting fish in a barrel.

Her logical mind would usually be trying to count steps or over-analyzing her movements, but somehow, with Chevy, her body surrendered to his lead, and she let him spin and steer her around the porch, one hand cupping her neck and the other cradling her outstretched palm.

He grinned down at her as he pulled her close and promenaded her in a circle. She felt dizzy and breathless—both from the dance steps and from Chevy's beaming smile that was meant just for her.

"My turn," Max called out, lifting his arms. "I want to dance, too."

Chevy laughed and let go of Leni to scoop up the little boy and spin him around, amazingly still in time with the music. Max giggled and whooped and sang along to the chorus with Chevy.

Leni leaned back against the front of the house, trying to catch her breath and calm her heart.

Sometimes, she forgot how much fun Chevy was. How he could turn anything into a party. He had a zeal for life—and probably a bit of a middle child's desire for attention—and had a way of taking the most menial task, like building railings for a set of steps, and turning it into something exciting and fun.

It was so easy to be around him, so easy to get pulled back into his orbit.

She had been on the shy side in high school, a brainy nerd who cared more about reading books than attending football games or parties. No one really paid much attention to her at all. Unless she was with Chevy.

There was something about him. About the way he was with her. Like he just *got* her. She didn't know how or why, but he saw beyond the nerdy brainiac and the quirky side of her.

They shouldn't have worked. The fun, loving cowboy who craved attention and the shy, timid bookworm who was happy to be on her own, escaping into her books and dreaming of dragons and time-travel and sci-fi adventures in space.

But they did.

He drew her out of her shell, and she made him laugh. And they just worked.

Right up until the day he'd broken her heart.

Chapter Twelve

Chevy's muscles burned as he swung the axe the next day, splitting the log with a satisfying whack. He swept the two pieces into the growing pile of firewood and grabbed another chunk of the tree that had fallen victim to a lightning bolt in a thunderstorm earlier that summer.

He'd come up to their family's cabin, tucked up into the mountains behind their ranch, to get away from everyone and have some time to think.

But his body and mind were restless, and chopping firewood always had a way of relieving stress for him.

Sweat dripped down his back as the afternoon sun beat down on his bare skin, his t-shirt discarded and tossed over the stacked pile to dry in the summer heat.

Frustration and exasperation fueled his next swing. He didn't know what was happening with Leni. She'd seemed happy to have him around the house the day—and the night—before but then something had happened after he'd danced with her on the porch.

It was like a cloud had crossed her face, and she went inside and didn't come back out again.

Lorna had told him she was upstairs working when they'd stopped for lunch and then again when he'd gone in to tell her that he and Dodge had finished the railings. It had taken them into the afternoon to sand and paint them, but they were sturdy, and no one would get a splinter when they ran their hand along them.

He'd texted Leni the night before. Just a simple message. *Hope you all are doing okay. Let me know if you need me or if I can do anything to help.*

She hadn't answered.

He'd lain awake half the night trying to think back over everything that had happened between them to see if he could figure out what he might have done to upset her. She was a little prickly at times, but then other times she was laughing and joking around with him. When she was first around him, her body was stiff, vibrating with tension. But then that night, in the dark comfort of her bed, her body—and her lips—had been pliant and warm as she'd melted into him.

The sound of an engine broke through the still air, and Chevy cocked his head to see if he recognized the vehicle. This engine was too quiet to be either his grandfather's or one of his brother's trucks.

A flash of dark metallic blue broke through the trees, and his heart leapt as he recognized Leni's Tesla. She must have finally picked it up from the library. He'd driven by it on his way home the night before, just to make sure it was okay, and that no one had messed with it.

Not that anyone would. Not in a town this size

where everyone knew who that fancy car belonged to.

He looked around for Murphy. The dog had run off into the woods to chase a squirrel, but the arrival of a vehicle usually brought the golden racing back.

His breath caught in his throat as Leni opened the door and stepped out. She was wearing a simple outfit of jean shorts, flip flops, and a black tank top. A delicate silver chain sparkled around her neck. Her dark hair was down, full and curly, the way he loved, and his palms itched to run his hands through it.

She pushed her sunglasses up on her head as she walked toward him, but he was already striding across the yard to get to her. They met in the middle, in front of the cabin, then stood awkwardly, staring at each other, like neither one knew quite what to say.

"Hi," he finally managed to get out.

She thrust the plastic container she was holding toward him. "I made you some cookies. To thank you. For the railings. And for everything you did to help us."

He took the container, surprised that she had baked him something after giving him the cold shoulder the day before. "Are these...?"

She nodded then almost begrudgingly admitted, "Yes. They're your favorite. The ones with the chocolate *and* the butterscotch chips."

He lifted the lid and groaned as he inhaled the buttery scents of vanilla, chocolate, and butterscotch. "My lord, these smell amazing." He lifted one out, took a big bite, and let out another groan. They were golden brown, baked to perfection, chewy on top, crispy on the bottom, the chips slightly melted from being in the sun, and as round as his fist. "These are so good," he said around a mouthful of cookie. Biting into it was like hearing an old favorite song on the radio, one that took him back to some of his happiest moments. "They taste like summer and make me think of that road trip we took to Salida to pick up that tractor part for Duke. You made a batch of these, and I think I ate half the container before we even made it out of town. That was a great trip."

"Okay. Don't get all worked up. They're just cookies."

"They're like heaven in my mouth." He took another one then closed the lid before he ate them all.

She laughed. "They're also kind of a peace offering. I'm sorry I ghosted you yesterday."

"What happened? I thought we were doing okay. Having fun."

"I don't know." She shrugged as she looked down at her feet, toeing a rock around with the edge of her sandal before looking back up at him. "I've been so mad at you. For years. And then, suddenly, I wasn't. I *was* having fun with you. And I liked being around you again. And it felt good. *Too* good. Because then I remembered that you broke my heart, and I just got mad all over again."

"Leni," he said, taking a step toward her. "I'm so sorry."

She held up a hand to stop whatever he was going to say next.

Which was actually okay, because he had no idea what he would have said. There was nothing to say.

No excuse. He had hurt her, and he'd done it on purpose.

He'd sent her away, forced her to leave this town and follow her dreams.

And the harsh reality was that he would do it again.

It didn't matter that it had torn his heart in two.

He hated that he'd hurt her, but she *had* left and gone to college at MIT and had gotten that aerospace engineering degree and a job at Boeing doing what she'd always dreamed about.

And that was worth the pain that it had caused him.

Because he would do anything to make her happy.

"Look, I just…" She swallowed as she stared at him, then waved her hand toward his chest. "Could you please put a shirt on. I can't talk to you when all your muscles are staring at me."

A grin broke across his face. *Sooo*, she liked his muscles.

He offered her a confused look as he lifted his arm like he was pointing at something but was really just flexing his bicep. "What muscles?" He did another exaggerated flex of both arms this time. "I don't know what you're talking about."

She covered her face with her hands. "Stop. I can't take it. When did you get so…" She paused, as if she couldn't come up with the right word. "So… muscle-y? And big? Do you work out now or something?"

He laughed again. "No. I just *work*. But on the ranch, I'm always lifting or hauling or carrying something, like bales of hay or baby calves." He flexed again, just to tease her. "So, I've come by these guns honestly."

She laughed with him. Finally, he'd made her laugh.

"Alright. But could you put your guns away. They're making me all...squirmy."

He liked making her squirmy.

"Fine. I'll just have to find my shirt. I think I left it over there." He flexed one more time as he pointed toward the woodpile but chuckled as he did it.

Before he could take a step forward, a streak of English cream came racing through the trees and sprinting toward them. Murphy ran straight for Leni then went crazy with seeing her—circling around her, tail wagging at a furious rate as he whined and rubbed against her legs, then rolled over on his belly in total golden retriever *I love you more than anything/ please pet me or I'll die* mode.

Chevy could understand why. He was pretty excited about seeing her too.

"Murphy." The word came out in a breathy whisper, then Leni laughed as she bent down to ruffle the dog's neck and rub his belly. "Oh my gosh. Murphy. I can't believe it. How are you, my sweet love?" She looked up at Chevy, who was feeling a little jealous at the affectionate endearments she was giving the dog. "Is this really Murphy? I can't believe you still have him."

"Yep, it's really him. He's an old man now, but he obviously remembers you." He laughed as Murphy covered Leni's face in puppy kisses. "He always loved you."

The dog wasn't the only one.

"Oh, you're such a good boy," she said, wrapping her arms around his neck as the dog put his paws up on her shoulders and knocked her over. She fell on her back, laughing as Murphy straddled her body, still wagging his tail as he licked her chin and face. "Gah, not my mouth," she said, still giggling as she tried to push his nose away from her face.

"Get off her, Murph," Chevy commanded as he hurried over to help. He grabbed Murphy's collar and tugged the dog back then reached his hand out to help pull Leni to her feet. "You okay?" he asked, brushing gravel and dust from her back.

"I'm fine," she said, still laughing. "It's been a long time since anyone's been that excited to see me."

"I felt that excited to see you when you drove up," he said, teasing her. "I just didn't wiggle my butt around as much. But I would have tackled you and covered you in kisses if I thought I could have gotten away with it."

She blinked up at him, her laughter gone, replaced with another look, one he couldn't be sure of. Was it longing? Affection? Annoyance?

She tore her gaze away and stared out over the lake in front of the cabin. "Wow, look at this place," she said, obviously changing the subject, although her voice still held a wistful tone. "I've got so many good memories of being here."

"Yeah?" He did too. And so many of them involved her. "Does it look any different?"

It had been over ten years since Leni had been there, and he dropped an arm casually around her shoulders as he stared out at the lake with her, taking in the view as if seeing it from her perspective.

The cabin was to the right. From the front, it probably hadn't changed much, same rough-hewn logs, same wide front porch with the two rocking chairs his grandfather had bought for his grandmother that faced the lake. Since Leni had been there, they'd added on an extra bedroom and updated the appliances and the plumbing, redoing the bathroom to add a tub and a nicer shower.

Most of the décor was the same, the curtains his grandma had made, the mountain landscape his great-grandfather had painted, the same tacky antler chandelier, and the baskets of pinecones that he and his brothers had probably collected when they were in grade school.

The lake was small, ringed with tall pine trees, with the side of the mountain climbing up about forty feet along its far side. A creek ran off the top of the ridge, forming a waterfall into the lake. A pine tree with heavy branches protruded over the side from the bank next to the cabin, and a rope swing hung over the water.

This afternoon, the water gently lapped at the shore, and he breathed in the scent of pine trees, wildflowers, and the lake.

He loved it here. It always felt like home. Even more so now…with Leni here.

"Maybe. The drive up felt the same, all those gorgeous sunflowers I love growing next to the road—those have always been my favorite."

"I remember." She'd almost always made him stop on the way down the mountain to pick a handful.

"But the trees seem taller. The cabin looks the same, although I remember it seeming bigger." She inhaled a deep breath, and her face broke into a smile. "But it smells the same. And the lake. Oh my gosh. The lake is still amazing. So beautiful. It's like a painting. Is the water still warm?"

Several hot springs in the mountains above the lake fed into it, so the water *was* truly warm.

"Go find out," he told her.

She looked at the water, then at him, then back at the water. Then she walked to the water's edge, kicked off her shoes, and waded in up to her knees. "Oh my gosh. It's amazing."

The water did look amazing, and he'd been dying for a swim all afternoon.

He shucked off his boots and jeans then let out a whoop as he raced past her, wearing only his black boxer briefs, and splashed into the water.

He ducked his head under then came up, shaking the water out of his hair. The temperature was perfect, warm but not hot, and cooler the deeper it went. He lifted his hand and beckoned her toward him. "Come on in. The water's fine."

"No way. I don't have a swimsuit."

He offered her one of his best flirty grins. "Never stopped you before."

She shifted from one foot to the other, chewing on her bottom lip.

"I know you're weighing the pros and cons in your head," he told her. It was what she'd always done.

She planted a hand on her hip. "You don't know me that well."

"Yeah, right. Go ahead. Lay them on me."

She let out a little indignant huff before starting the list. "The biggest pro is that the water looks incredible, and I'm hot and could practically die from wanting to go for a swim."

"Avoiding dying seems like a pretty big *pro*. What kind of con could possibly challenge that?"

"Wellll, the biggest one is that getting in the water means I'd have to take my clothes off."

"Nope. That definitely goes in the *pro* column for me." He waggled his eyebrows playfully at her. "Oh, come on. You've got nothing I haven't seen before."

"Oh yes, I have. I have *much* more now than you've seen before. I'm no longer a seventeen-year-old girl with flawless skin and no dimples or cellulite. My body has changed. I am much…" She paused as if struggling to come up with the best descriptive word. "Much *curvier* now."

"I happen to like your new curves. In fact, the curvier the better I like to say."

"Oh yeah? When do you like to say that?"

"Just now. And also, any time there's a possibility of a gorgeous, curvy woman, stripping naked in front of me." He offered her another one of his trademark grins—the one that most women couldn't resist.

But most women weren't Eleanor Gibbs.

She was different.

"Tell you what," he said. "How about if I turn my back, and I won't look while you strip down and wade in."

She twisted her mouth from side-to-side with indecision. "You promise you won't look?"

He held up two fingers. "Scout's honor."

She arched an eyebrow. "Now I know you're lyin'. You were never a Boy Scout."

He laughed. "Okay. I promise I won't look…*after* your shirt and shorts come off."

She huffed again.

"Come on, darlin'," he drawled. "You gotta give me a little something here."

"No, I don't." She tried to keep the annoyed expression on her face but couldn't hold it as she broke into a laugh.

He splashed a small spray of water in her direction then held up three fingers. "All right, you had your chance to do this the easy way. Now, Miss Eleanor Gibbs, you've got exactly three seconds to peel those clothes off, or I'm coming out of this lake to do it for you."

Chapter Thirteen

Leni narrowed her eyes at him. "You wouldn't dare."

Oh, he *would* dare. In fact, he couldn't *wait* to dare. Chevy took a step toward her as he called out, "Three!"

She let out a shriek as she retreated up the shore, splashing water as she walked backward.

His grin widened as he took another menacing step toward her. "Two!"

"Okay, you win. Stop counting." She laughed as she shimmied out of her shorts and tossed them further back onto the bank, then pulled her shirt over her head and pitched it toward the shorts, leaving her in only a black lacy bra and a pair of black bikini panties. She made a circular motion with her hand. "Now, turn around."

He stared, the sight of her half-naked body making his mouth go dry.

The last time he'd seen her like this, she *was* seventeen, and he was a horn-dog teenage boy. Now, she was a full-fledged woman, round and lush, and as his gaze roamed over those curves she'd described, he felt like that love-sick out-of-control teenager again.

"Why are you staring at me?" she asked, self-consciously putting her hands up to cover herself.

"I can't help it," he said, all teasing aside. "You're just so gorgeous."

A grin tugged at the corners of her lips. "Stop it."

"It's true."

"You're just trying to get me to take my bra off in front of you."

He shook his head, trying to keep the sincerity in his voice. "No, it's true. You're beautiful." He couldn't help the grin that creased his face. "Although, if you *do* want to take your bra off in front of me..."

She playfully kicked water at him with her foot. "Turn around, Lassiter."

"Okay, okay." He dutifully turned his back to her, but his stomach pitched as he heard the scrap of fabric land on her pile of clothes and the soft splashes as she quickly waded into the water behind him.

"You can look now," she said, as she swam past him and out into the lake.

Her bare shoulders were the only thing visible above the water but knowing she was topless under the surface was enough to drive him mad.

She dipped her head under the water then let out a whoop as she came back out. "This feels amazing," she shouted into the sky.

They spent the next hour swimming around, splashing and teasing and making each other laugh.

It had felt so good to be with her again, that Chevy hadn't been paying attention to the dark clouds rolling in over the mountain until they suddenly blocked the sun.

"Dang. Those clouds look ominous," he said, studying the sky. "We'd better get out."

They started swimming for shore. But when they got closer, Leni stopped and pointed to the bank. "Um, Chev...do you happen to know where my clothes went?"

He waded into the shallow water, searching the bank for her shorts and top. He spotted one flip flop next to her pair of shorts, but they weren't where she'd left them. "I'm pretty sure that guy you were uttering all those sweet nothings to earlier took off with most of your clothes. Your shorts are still here and one shoe though." He whistled for the dog. "Murphy, get back here."

The dog came running around the side of the cabin, Leni's black lacy bra clutched in his mouth.

"Give me that," Chevy said, holding out his hand as he walked toward the dog. The rocks got thicker and sharper, the further he got out of the water, and he grimaced as they bit into his feet with each step.

The dog must have mistaken his menacing tone for one of playfulness, because he took off, racing back and forth across the bank as Chevy tried to grab Leni's bra while not breaking his toe on one of the rocks. "Forget this," he muttered as he grabbed his boots and yanked them on.

Little grains of dirt still bit into the soles of his feet since he hadn't wiped them off in his haste to pull on his boots, but it was better than the jagged rocks on the bank.

"There he goes," Leni called as the dog raced by him again. "Grab him, Chev."

"I'm trying," he said, racing back and forth as the dog dodged this way and that and then sprinted away, the strap of Leni's bra dragging in the dirt as he ran. He tried not to think about what an idiot he must look like running around in just his boots and his underwear. He turned back to Leni. "Just how badly do you need that bra?"

She didn't answer. Her gaze had dropped to his boxer briefs and from the way she was staring, the soaking wet fabric apparently left little to her imagination.

Just knowing she was looking—and seemingly not able to pull her gaze away—added to the fact that she was naked in the water and the dog had run off with the majority of her clothes had his mind going to all sorts of dark places. And suddenly the part she was staring at decided to stand at attention.

A flash of lightning lit up the air, followed immediately by a deafening clap of thunder.

All thoughts of them both being half-naked left his mind as alarm filled his chest, and he yelled, "Leni, get out of the water! Now!"

Her eyes widened. They both knew how quickly a thunderstorm could roll in over the mountains and the damage that lightning could do. She stumbled forward, grabbing for her shorts and the lone sandal, wincing as the rocks bit into her feet.

He raced toward her as another flash of lightning struck, this one even closer. It lit up the sky as the thunder cracked at the same time.

The clouds opened up just as he reached her and let loose a torrential downpour.

The hard rain pelted his skin as he bent and scooped her up, shielding her body with his as he sprinted toward the cabin. "Murphy, come!" he yelled for the dog, but his voice got swallowed in the deafening sound of the rain.

Turning the knob, he flung the door open and ran inside. The dog darted in after him, Leni's bra still dangling from his mouth. Chevy slammed the door and leaned his forehead down to meet Leni's, his breath ragged as he cradled her against his bare chest.

She had one arm clinging to his neck and the other across her chest as she tried to cover herself with the tiny pair of shorts and the lone sandal.

Another flash of lightning and more thunder rumbled across the sky, but Chevy barely noticed. He only had eyes for the woman clutched in his arms. They were both drenched. Water dripped from her hair and skin, soaking the rug inside the door.

"You all right?" he asked, his voice low and hoarse from shouting.

She dipped her chin, a barely perceptible nod. Her eyes were still wide as she stared up at him, her lips parted. "I'm okay," she whispered as the subtle scent of her hair surrounded him.

He knew what he should do. He *should* carry her to the sofa, put her down, and cover her with a blanket. But her body was warm against his, and she was practically naked, the side of her lush breast pressing into the bare skin of his chest.

Aw hell. He'd never been good at following the rules.

He leaned in and captured her perfect mouth in a kiss.

Chapter Fourteen

Heat surged through Chevy's veins as Leni kissed him back, her fingers digging into his neck as she pulled him closer. But it wasn't enough. He needed to get his hands on her, to fill his palms with her luscious ass.

When they'd redone the kitchen, they had put in a large island with a black pebbled leather countertop. With a few long strides, and still kissing her, Chevy carried Leni forward then set her on the island.

Within seconds of her butt hitting the counter, her legs were wrapped around his waist, and she let out a moan as she ground her hips into his.

He was already hard as a rock, the cold rain on his skin forgotten, as he pulled back to look down at her. She braced one hand behind her on the counter, giving him a full view of her sumptuous body. Everything about her was voluptuous, from her full hips to her round breasts to her pink-tipped nipples. He dipped his head, sucking one pert bud into his mouth and circling it with his tongue.

She moaned as he reached to fill his palm with her other breast, grazing that nipple with his thumb as he continued to sample the other. Arching her back, she gave more of herself to him, and he took it, greedy to caress and touch, to kiss and caress.

This was more of her than he'd had in years, but it still wasn't enough.

He needed to taste her.

Hooking his thumb under the waistband of her bikinis, he drew her panties down her legs and let them drop to the floor. Then he laid a trail of kisses across her belly then into the dip next to her hip.

Going to his knees, he spread her legs and continued his onslaught of kisses, trailing his tongue along her inner thigh, teasing and skimming his teeth against her skin until finally, he claimed her with his mouth.

His name escaped her lips, a whispered word on the edge of a moan as she writhed against him. And the sound of it almost sent him over the edge.

He wanted to please her, to make her not just whisper, but scream his name. His skills had improved since he was a fumbling teenager, and he used all of them now, his mouth and his hand to caress and rub, tease and stroke, until her back was arching, and her hands were gripping the sides of the island as she shuddered out her release.

He stood and kissed her again, softly this time as he wrapped his hands around her back and pulled her body against his bare chest. Hugging her to him, his face now buried in the silky softness of her hair. "You okay?" he whispered.

"I will be, as long as you tell me there's at least one condom somewhere in this cabin."

He laughed as he pulled back to look at her. "Only one?"

"One to start," she said, her smile coy as she peered up at him from under her long, thick eyelashes.

A slow smile spread across his face. "In that case, I'll tear this place apart to find one or use a Ziploc bag and a rubber band if I have to, because darlin', I think I might die if I don't have you soon."

"Didn't you tell me earlier that avoiding dying seemed like a pretty big item in the pro column?"

"I did indeed."

"Then you'd better start looking." She laughed as he picked her up again and this time, carried her into the bedroom. He pulled back the quilt and top sheet before setting her on the bed, then he yanked open the top drawer of the nightstand, praying one of his brothers had at some point left a stash here.

He had one in his wallet, but he'd left it and his phone on the seat of his pickup. Although he'd challenge the storm and run back through the downpour to retrieve it if he had to.

Thankfully he didn't have to.

"Yes, found some," he cried, holding up a strip of several square packets.

"And more than one," she said, another one of those coy grins crossing her face as she lay back against the bed, brazenly displaying her luscious body, her dark hair, still damp and smelling like rain, spread out over the pillow. Apparently, she'd learned a few things since they were teenagers, too.

He shucked off his boxer briefs, and she pulled him down onto the bed then climbed on top of him, straddling his waist, her shoulders back, as if offering him a perfect view of her delicious body. And he was soaking in every square inch of it.

She was sexy in a new way—more sensuous—like she knew the power her body had over him and how to use that power to drive him insane.

Being with her was both familiar and all new—and exciting as hell.

This time he groaned her name as she moved her hips, rolling and grinding against him, bringing herself pleasure as she tormented him in the most exquisite way. He let her, savoring her attention and indulging in the bliss of just being able to look at her, to touch and caress.

Then he couldn't take it anymore. He flipped her over and took his fill once again of her lush breasts, kissing and nipping, circling the tightened tips with his tongue, teasing her until she writhed beneath him, then he tore open a foil packet and covered himself before parting her legs and burying himself inside her.

Chapter Fifteen

Afterwards, Leni lay in the crook of Chevy's arm, their legs tangled together, smiling as she traced her finger along the muscled bicep she'd been admiring earlier.

The storm had passed, and the sun shining through the bedroom window warmed her bare shoulder.

She still couldn't quite believe what had just happened. Had she really gone skinny-dipping with Chevy Lassiter then let him take her to O-town on the edge of his kitchen island?

Then again in his bed?

Then still again?

This was not like her. She hadn't skinny-dipped since she was eighteen years old. Although technically, she'd left her underwear on, so she wasn't sure it even counted as the skinny part.

When she'd decided to go for a swim, she'd planned to leave both her undies and her bra on. But then Chevy had teased and flirted with her, and it felt like she was eighteen again, and suddenly she was unsnapping her bra and tossing it to the ground.

The warm water had felt delicious on her skin,

and swimming around with Chevy knowing she was topless had been a crazy turn-on. Maybe that's why she'd acted so out of character once they got inside the cabin.

Vanilla was her normal relationship lane. She didn't do hot crazy sex. In fact, she hadn't had *any* sex in months, let alone the insane kind. And especially not with men she barely knew.

Although Chevy *wasn't* someone she barely knew. He'd been the love of her life. The one she still dreamed of in the quiet moments when she let herself remember his smile.

Still, even with the hardware engineer from Lockheed Martin that she'd dated for six months, she'd never acted in bed the way she had with Chevy—with such reckless abandon.

Something had come over her. She didn't know if it was the rain or the storm or the fact that she was half-naked and in the arms of the only man she'd ever really given her heart to.

She was only planning to be here for a few weeks, so maybe it just felt like she had this one chance, this one opportunity to be with him. Or maybe it was because it all felt so good, kissing him again, the delicious way he teased her, that something in her just gave in and surrendered to his touch.

She'd never felt so brazen, so wanton, but it had been so freeing, and so much fun.

Although now that it was over, and the sun was shining and they weren't in the dark cabin, dripping wet, with a storm flashing and crashing around them, she suddenly felt shy. And more than a little awkward.

Would he think she always acted like that?

"I should probably get back," she told him. She'd been gone for hours.

"I'm surprised you were able to stay for so long. How'd you get away this afternoon?"

"Maisie stopped by and said she'd stay for the afternoon. She's really sweet. She brought a plate of brownies and a stack of books for Max and one for her and Lorna. I think the three of them were planning to read all afternoon."

He rolled onto his side to face her and ran his finger along the tiny dent next to her collarbone, sending a shiver down her spine. "Then it sounds like you have time to stay a little longer."

Heat coiled in her belly as she smiled at him. "I should probably at least check in. I told her I was coming up here, so I'm sure she's not worried, but my phone is still in my purse in the car, so I don't know if she's tried to text me."

"How *did* you know I was up here?"

"Duke dropped off a pan of chicken enchiladas and happened to mention that you were spending the afternoon at the cabin."

"Just happened to mention it, huh?"

"Yes, come to think of it, it did feel a little like he tried to stick that information into the conversation."

"I'm glad he did."

Murphy padded into the bedroom, jumped up on the bed, and laid down, his head resting on Leni's ankle.

Chevy gestured to the dog. "You're gonna have to convince Murphy to give you back your bra if you plan to go anywhere."

"What good is my bra if I don't have a shirt?"

"You're right. There's no point. We should just stay naked and in bed for the rest of the day."

She laughed. Although that wasn't a bad idea.

He gestured to the window. "With the kind of storm we just had, there's a good chance the road is flooded, so you probably won't be able to leave anyway."

"Oh no." Her Tesla was a great car, but it didn't have a lot of clearance when it came to dirt roads. "Do you really think it's washed out?"

He shrugged. "Probably. It usually is when it rains that hard. But it normally only takes a few hours for the water to recede then it's passable again." He slid his hand under the sheets and along her thigh. "I've got a few ideas of some things we could in that time."

Just the slightest touch of his hand and heat and need were already building between her legs.

It would be so easy. Just lean in to kiss him. But would they be able to recapture the lust and passion they'd just created during the storm? She wasn't sure.

They had just spent several hours together naked and doing lots of those 'ideas' he'd just mentioned. So, why was she suddenly feeling awkward and embarrassed?

Maybe because she hadn't seen this man or talked to him in the better part of a decade. Then within days of being around him again, she'd fallen into bed with him.

Although he had been there for her during the emergency situation with her sister, *and* he'd taken care of Isabel and Max. Cradling that tiny baby against his chest was one of the most swoon-worthy things she'd ever seen. If she hadn't been in crisis-mode, she might have climbed him like a tree right then.

He'd also built Lorna a set of railings.

Wearing a tool belt. Don't forget the tool belt.

That heat was getting more intense just thinking about it.

Plus, he was Chevy. The boy—man, *gulp*—who she had grown up with, that she had given her heart, *and her virginity*, too. He wasn't a random stranger she'd picked up in a bar.

He was part of her history, part of her heart.

Still, things were moving pretty fast. They seemed to have skipped the 'catching up' phase of seeing each other again and went straight from the crazy night of a crisis into falling into bed together. Except they hadn't really fallen, it was more like they'd hurtled headlong into a passion-fueled collision. Like all the systems in her brain had crashed, and her body had just taken over like some crazy sex-starved virus.

Except, if her computer or her systems at her job failed, or got infected with a virus, she knew what to do. She knew how to analyze a problem, figure out a solution or a formula that made sense.

But none of this made any sense.

She dealt with facts and figures, with numbers and science. This was all emotion and feelings. She couldn't just turn those off and then turn them back on again.

Although the way Chevy's hand was sliding along her thigh seemed to suggest that she could be turned back on again. And quite easily.

She let out a sigh, that rational part of her brain

trying to take back control. "I really should get back. I'd hate to think Lorna might have needed me, and I haven't been answering my phone or texts in hours."

"Yeah, I get that. And my phone's in the pickup, so even if she'd tried mine, I haven't answered either," he said, dropping his hand and throwing back the sheet. "Let me find some dry stuff to wear, and I'll go outside and try to track down what Doofus did with your shoe and the rest of your clothes."

"I'd appreciate that," she said, giving the dog, who had crawled into the empty spot next to Leni that Chevy had vacated, a cuddle.

"We usually leave some extra stuff up here." He crossed to the dresser, found a pair of gray sweatpants, and pulled them on. He was going commando, and she swallowed at the sight of him. The thin sweatpants left nothing to the imagination as he continued to dig through the drawer, coming up with a flannel shirt that he tossed on the bed. "You can wear this." He offered her a wolfish grin. "Although I prefer you in your current state, but if you insist on getting dressed, at least this should hold you until your clothes are dry."

She laughed. "I do, in fact, insist." She pulled on the flannel, rolling up the sleeves, and buttoning a few of the buttons. Her legs were bare as she padded into the front room of the cabin to find her shorts and hunt down what the dog did with her bra.

Spotting her underwear on the floor in the kitchen, she bent over to retrieve them and heard a groan from behind her.

"Damn, woman. You're killin' me all over again.

You look sexy as hell in my shirt, but then you bent over and gave me a peek at that gorgeous ass of yours and about sent me into cardiac arrest."

She laughed as she strode over to where her shorts were and bent forward to grab them, offering Chevy another risqué glimpse, and earned another moan from him.

Where had this shameless woman come from?

She'd just been thinking about how awkward and shy she'd suddenly felt in the bedroom, then a little encouragement from Chevy, and she's bending over and flashing him her cheeky bits.

She normally tried to hide her butt and certainly never flaunted any part of herself, especially in naked form. But he made her feel beautiful. And sexy. It was the way he looked at her. And he made it so fun to tease him.

"Found your bra," he said, holding it up by one strap. "It may have gotten a little slobbered on though, so I'd suggest not bothering to even put it on."

She laughed. "You are shameless."

He shrugged, not troubled at all by her remark, as he pulled on his boots.

"Was the one you gave me the only shirt in that drawer?" she asked, glancing at this bare chest and trying not to drool.

"Probably not," he said with a wink and another grin before he walked out the front door.

She took advantage of his absence to run to the bathroom and wash her face. She was a mess. Her hair was a crazy tangle of curls, and she tried to finger-comb out the worst of it. Finding some toothpaste in a drawer, she swished some around in her mouth, rubbing it onto her teeth with her tongue before rinsing it out.

She heard the door open and close, and she came out of the bathroom to see Chevy holding up her flip flop.

"Found your sandal, but no luck tracking down your top. I'll keep looking."

She shrugged. "It's not a big deal. It's one of a few I bought from Walmart last night after realizing I was staying longer than I'd planned. And I'm sure it will eventually turn up."

"I'll buy you a new one." He glared at the dog who had followed Leni into and out of the bathroom and was now lying at her feet. "And I'll take it out of Murphy's dog treat budget."

The dog let out a groan as if he'd understood Chevy's threat.

Leni's underwear had been dry, so she'd pulled those back on, but the denim shorts were still damp and the thought of putting on a slobbery bra made her grimace, so she just slipped her sandals on with the flannel shirt and hoped she could sneak into the house that way without her sister catching her coming home braless and in someone else's shirt.

"I'll call you later," Chevy said, pulling her to him to kiss her goodbye. "Or call me if you need anything. I can always run into town. I mean it. For anything."

"Thanks," she told him, and wasn't sure what else to say.

This whole afternoon had felt surreal, and now that she was getting ready to go back into the real world, her old insecurities were rearing their ugly heads.

Her brow furrowed as she peered up at him. "You're

not seeing anyone else right now, are you? I mean, not that *we're* seeing each other, or that I'm expecting anything, but I guess, I'm asking..." She was royally screwing this up. It was hard to believe she led whole teams of people and explained complicated formulas to other engineers. *Just spit it out.* "Do you currently have a girlfriend or someone that you're dating?"

His eyes widened. "What? No. Geez. Do you think I would have done that..." He tilted his head toward the bedroom. "Or *that*..." Heat warmed the back of her neck as he gestured toward the kitchen island. "...if I was seeing someone else?" His eyes narrowed. "Why? Do *you* have a boyfriend."

She huffed out a laugh. "Um. No. Not in a very long time. I'm mostly married to my job."

He nodded. "Good. Well, I don't have a girlfriend either. And I'm not with anyone else. Although I am hoping to say that I'm seeing someone *now*." He lowered his head and offered her a sidelong glance, as if afraid of the answer to the question he was covertly asking.

Did this all mean they were seeing each other now? Did she *want* them to be *seeing* each other?

She certainly didn't want to *see* anyone else.

But that didn't mean she was ready to go 'all in' and commit to getting back together with Chevy Lassiter.

Apparently, her mouth hadn't been paying attention to what her mind was thinking, because it blurted out, "Yes. You are *seeing* someone now. And I'll *see* you later." She gave him another quick kiss then slipped out the door.

She got to her car and slid into the driver's seat, the

flannel shirt barely covering her tush, and the leather seat was warm on the back of her legs. Digging through her purse, she found her phone and checked the display. No messages from her sister.

She sent Lorna a quick text. "Everything okay?"

"Yep. All good," came her sister's reply. "You okay?"

"Yep. All good too."

Better than good.

"And how is Chevy? Did you find him? You've been gone for hours. Did anything pop up for you to talk about?"

Her sister followed her message with an eggplant emoji, and Leni laughed out loud. Her phone dinged again, this time with just the emoji of a taco. Then another text with just a peach.

Leni cracked up as she typed back, "We're working through some things." She added a winky face. Although she could have created the story of the whole afternoon with images of a lake, a dog, a bra, a lightning bolt, a peach, a bed, and *several* eggplants.

"Maisey is here, and Elizabeth just stopped by with chips and salsa to go with the enchiladas, so no need to rush home. Unless you're hungry. Otherwise, stay as long as you want."

She looked down the road then back at the cabin. Chevy had said the gravel road was *probably* washed out. She weighed the risk of it against the benefit of what was back in the cabin.

It couldn't hurt to give it a *little* longer for the water to dry. It certainly wasn't worth getting stuck. Not when there was a six-foot-something, broad-shouldered alternative waiting for her inside.

"The storm flooded the road to the cabin, so I

might stay a little longer to let it dry out," she typed. "Go ahead and eat without me. I'm not hungry."

Not for chips and salsa anyway.

Dropping her phone into her purse, she brought it with her as she walked back to the cabin, her stomach full of butterflies at the thought of being with Chevy again.

She felt like a skydiver standing at the open door of the plane, anxious and terrified, but also excited, her whole body tingling and wired at the anticipation of experiencing that thrilling free fall into the sky.

"Hey," he said, a slow grin crossing his face as she walked through the door. "You're back."

"I started to leave, but you're right, it's better to wait for the road to dry out." She was already unbuttoning the flannel shirt and stepping out of her sandals. "And I was thinking about some of those *ideas* you had about how we could fill the time," she said as she let the shirt drop to the floor.

Chapter Sixteen

LENI JUGGLED A drink carrier holding coffees for her and her sister with her purse as she walked out of Mountain Brew a few days later. Her mind was on a hundred different things, from taking care of her sister and the store to what she was going to feed Max for supper and always with underlying thoughts of Chevy.

What was he doing? What was he thinking?

What was *she* doing with him?

And why had her giant logical brain turned to mush so that she couldn't get through an hour without thinking about him?

She hadn't seen the tall cowboy the day before. He and his brothers had spent most of it moving a herd of cattle from one pasture to another and then catching up on chores when they got back that night.

But he had texted her a few times throughout the day, and every time her phone had buzzed in her pocket, she'd gotten a thrill of anticipation at what he might have to say.

His messages had all been sweet, asking how her

day was going or just telling her he was thinking about her.

They were supposed to get together that night. He was picking her up at six and taking her out for barbecue at the Tipsy Pig. But first, she needed to bring her sister this decaf skinny iced caramel macchiato and shower off the scent of coffee in her hair.

Her car was parked on the street in front of the shop, and her heart swelled as she saw the handful of sunflowers that she was sure a certain handsome cowboy had picked and put under her windshield wipers.

She called Chevy as she drove back to Lorna's. "Thanks for the flowers. They're gorgeous," she said as soon as he picked up.

"What flowers?" he asked. "Is some guy giving you flowers? Tell me his name, and I'll kick his ass."

"Very funny." She couldn't remember the last time a man had bought her flowers. Or picked some for her from the side of the road.

"I'm glad you like them. From your text earlier, it sounded like you were having a rough day. We've got a sick calf, so I had to run into town real quick to grab some antibiotics. I knew I wouldn't have time to stop for more than a minute, and I saw the sunflowers and thought they might make you smile."

"They did." Although seeing him would have made her even happier. "Next time, text me and I'll run you out a coffee."

"I was gonna poke my head in, but I could see a line of people through the window and just didn't have the time to wait."

"Yeah. It felt like we were busy for most of the day. Is the calf okay?"

He let out a weary sigh. "He will be."

"You sound tired. Are you sure you're up for coming into town for supper?"

"Heck yeah. I *am* tired, but I'm not gonna miss out on a date with the hottest aerospace engineer in town. I may come home early and hit the sack though. We're moving cattle again tomorrow, so I need to be up before the sun."

"More cattle?" She didn't remember them having that big of a herd.

"Yeah, we made the decision to get a hundred extra head this year. It should pay off in the end, but it's a lot of extra work, especially with Ford spending so much time working on his and Elizabeth's farm too. But Gramps has a buddy, Bucky Ferguson...not sure if you remember him, he and his wife have that place up the canyon. He used to drive that old blue pickup with the one gray fender."

"Sure, I remember Bucky. His wife worked at the school."

"Yeah, that's him. Anyway, his son has a big outfit in Texas, and he told Bucky he could spare a guy to send up here for a few months to help with the corn harvest and to get in our winter wheat. And we could sure use the help to wean calves and move all those cattle from the summer pastures to the winter ones. Plus, we've got fences to mend and plenty of maintenance crap we've been neglecting since we were so busy with calving in the spring."

"Sounds like it's a good thing you're getting some help. When's he supposed to arrive?"

"Not sure. Soon as Bucky's boy can spare him. Hopefully soon."

"Yes, I hope so. I hate hearing that stress in your voice."

"I'll be fine. This is the life of a rancher. Always another chore to do."

"I'm at the house, so I'll let you go," she told him, pulling into the driveway. "See you in a few hours. And thanks again for the flowers."

"Sure thing, darlin'. See you soon."

"I'm home," she called out as she walked through the front door and deposited everything onto the kitchen counter.

Max came racing into the kitchen to crash into her, and she bent down to let him wrap his arms around her neck as she squeezed him tight. There is nothing like a hug from a five-year-old to make the stress of a rough day melt away.

She arranged the sunflowers in a vase before carrying the iced coffees and a plate of cookies into the back room where her sister was nursing Isabel and concentrating on the notes she was furiously taking in a notebook.

"Thanks sis. You are the best," Lorna said, taking a bite of a cookie and a big sip of the coffee then letting out a long sigh. "That is so good. And I'm just going to pretend there is caffeine in it."

"What are you working on?" Leni asked, perching on the side of the sofa.

Izzy had apparently finished because Lorna handed her to Leni to burp as she pulled her clothes back together. "With everything that's happened, I'd almost forgotten about the festival this weekend."

"What festival?" Leni asked, her focus more on balancing her niece on her knee and positioning the palm of her hand in the right spot on her belly. Izzy gurgled as she leaned forward, her head hanging over the top of Leni's left hand while she used her right to pat the baby's tiny back.

"Oh, come on, you haven't been gone *that* long. The *Beans, Brews, and Bands* festival."

"Do they still do that thing?" Of course Leni remembered the annual chili cook-off. The majority of the businesses in town participated, creating their own recipes for chili that they passed samples of out to festivalgoers who then rated and judged their favorites. Two of the local breweries sold beer and wine, and they had several bands that played music throughout the day.

It was a summertime favorite in Woodland Hills, and the whole county showed up.

"Yes, of course they still do it," Lorna said.

Izzy let out a good burp, almost as if she'd had one of the brews from the festival. "Good girl," Leni told her then looked back up at her sister, still not getting the significance. "So, why do you care so much about the festival? Did you have tickets to go to it or something?"

"No, I don't have tickets to *go*. Mountain Brew is one of the participants. This is the second year we've had a booth, and last year, we almost took the title of Best Chili."

"Wait? You mean you set up a stand and hand out chili samples?"

"Heck yeah, I do. Or I'm supposed to. And last year, we killed it with sales of iced tea and lemonade. We had these special water bottles made with our logos on them, and we sold them for fifteen bucks a pop and earned ten dollars profit on each one. Last year, we cleared over two thousand dollars before selling out right after lunch, so this year I went all in, got an even better deal on the water bottles and ordered five times as many."

Leni frowned. "Yikes. That's a bummer. But I guess you can just save them for next year."

"No, you're not getting it. We're still doing the booth."

"Who's *we*? You and your trusty knee-scooter, Betty?"

Her sister gave her one of those stares that meant serious business. "No. I mean *we* as in *you and me*. And Emily, I guess," she said referring to the Johnson girl who worked at the shop. "And anyone else I can talk into helping us."

"Are you serious? You still want to try to make chili, run a booth, and sell a thousand water bottles of iced tea and lemonade?"

Lorna nodded. "And I've also been thinking about asking you to make a bunch of your cookies, individually wrapping them, slapping our stickers on the front, and selling those too. I looked on Amazon, and we can get the cello bags by tomorrow, and I'm sure our little print shop could easily make me a couple hundred stickers by then too."

Leni almost choked, and she was sure she was bug-eyed as she stared at her sister. "You *must* be joking now. You want me to make *two hundred* cookies by *this* weekend? Like, you know today is Wednesday, and the festival is what? On Saturday?"

❖

Lorna nodded. "We've still got tonight and two full days, and I know how you love to plan and execute a project. We can get the ingredients tomorrow. And I already called Elizabeth, and she said she'd love to help at the coffee shop on Friday, so you can have the whole day off to bake." She frowned again. "Although we're going to have to make the chili that day too."

"And we're going to accomplish this all with your broken ankle and nursing a newborn baby? You're crazy."

"Maybe, but that's never stopped us from pulling a plan together before," Lorna said. "Remember when we arranged that whole surprise birthday party for Mom's 40th? You didn't believe we could pull that off either, and yet we still had a bouncy house, a chocolate fountain, and Mom's favorite band set up in our backyard."

Leni laughed. "That was a fun night."

"Come on. We can do it," Lorna said, a pleading tone in her voice. "I'm not totally helpless. I can sit at the kitchen table and put stickers on the bags and stuff cookies in them."

"Well then, that's practically everything."

Her sarcasm was not lost on her sister.

"Will this be tough? Yes. But I promise it will be doable." Lorna held up her notebook. "I've been working on a plan and a schedule all afternoon. We can't make the lemonade and iced tea until the night before, but I've already got multiple huge ten-gallon water coolers for the drinks and several five-gallon buckets purchased to put the chili in. The chili we give away for free, but we just do small samples, so we don't have to make as much as you'd think. I've already placed an ice order with the grocery store for Saturday, and I got the water bottles months ago, so those have already been washed and are ready to fill."

"Sounds like you've thought of everything."

"Everything except how to find a few more volunteers to help us."

"Do you want me to ask Chevy and his family? He told me he would do anything for me. I'm not sure he knew that meant baking two-hundred cookies and making a ten-gallon vat of chili, but I'd bet he'll still be willing to help."

"That would be great. Except the Lassiter Ranch has their own booth. They're the ones who took the winning prize last year."

Chapter Seventeen

Their date night at the Tipsy Pig wasn't quite the romantic evening Leni had envisioned. Although how romantic could a date be when they were slurping barbeque sauce off chicken wings and listening to the old nineties music someone kept choosing on the jukebox.

She had laid out Lorna's plans to Chevy, and just like she'd thought, he'd instantly agreed to help.

"But what about your family's booth?" she asked.

Chevy shrugged as he took a swig of beer. "We'll be fine. Duke's already been working on his chili recipe. He's made us six different versions over the summer. And I think if we set up our stalls next to each other, the guys and I should be able to help with both booths. I think Maisie might be doing a booth for the library, so she's out, but we've got Elizabeth to help this year, too." He waved a chicken wing at her. "It'll be fine. I can come over the night before and help with the cookies, too. And we'll use my pickup to load all your stuff and take it to the fairgrounds Saturday morning. Although, come to think of it, last year, they let us set up our tents on Friday night. That would help if they did that again this year."

She stared at him. "The idea of this doesn't make you anxious?" She'd spent her whole time in the shower running numbers in her head and trying to figure out the logistics of how to make this massive thing happen.

"No way. This'll be fun." He offered her a casual shrug. "Don't worry. It will all work out."

***

"I thought you said this would all work out," Leni practically shrieked into the phone that Saturday morning as Chevy was loading his truck with the canopy tent they planned to use for their booth.

"And it all still will," he told her.

"Oh really? Because nothing has so far. I burned two batches of cookies yesterday because I was trying to help put stickers on five million cello baggies, I accidentally put a cup of sugar into my chili instead of salt, and Max lost his shit when he left one of his favorite Legos on the stove and it thermally reconfigured."

"What the hell does that mean?"

"In layman's terms, it means it melted."

He let out a laugh. "Poor Max. Why was that particular Lego his favorite?"

"I'm not sure. He just kept saying 'but that was a blue one'."

"Gotcha," he said, making a mental note to search

Amazon to try to find Max some new blue Legos. "But the cookies all got finished, and your idea to make bone-shaped biscuits for the dogs at the festival was pure genius. Every dog lover is going to vote for your chili on principal alone. And who knows, maybe adding that sugar will be the winning ingredient that puts you in first place."

"Do you understand how chemistry works at all? You can't just sub out sucrose for sodium chloride and think you'll get the same result."

"I don't know," he said, continuing to load the truck. "Sweet and salty is a thing. Maybe a stressed-out night in the kitchen and an accidental ingredient swap is how kettle corn was invented."

She laughed. "You're a dork."

"Yeah," he agreed. "But at least I made you laugh."

"Just like you always do."

The sound of her laughter, especially when he was the one responsible for it, was the best thing in the world. And something he'd missed. He still couldn't believe that Leni Gibbs was back in his life. That he was able to kiss her and hold her hand and hell, just the fact that they were texting and talking on the phone again was incredible.

"Hey, I gotta go," he told her. "I've got to finish packing the truck up, and then Murph and I are heading your way. Gramps and Dodge already left for the fairgrounds, and Ford and Elizabeth are planning to meet us there. Try to get everything into the driveway, and I should be there within fifteen minutes."

"We'll be ready."

"See you soon. And try not to worry." He heard

her laugh again as he hung up the phone and shoved it into his pocket.

A white pickup came down the driveway and pulled up next to him as he was tying down the rest of the supplies for the festival.

He noted the dead bugs dotting the windshield and the Texas plates. This had to be the guy Gramps had told them about. The one Bucky Ferguson said his son was sending.

A tall, dark-haired guy in jeans and a straw cowboy hat got out of the truck and ambled toward him. His square-toed boots had the dust and wear of ones that had truly been worked in, and he had a multi-tool attached to the side of his leather belt. He wore a champion buckle, but nothing too big or flashy. He looked to be about Dodge's age, but the scruff of his beard might be making him look older.

"You the guy from Texas?" Chevy asked, pulling on a knot.

The cowboy frowned then nodded slowly. "Yeah, I just drove up from the Panhandle."

"Great. We heard you were comin'."

The guy scratched the back of his neck. "You did?"

"Yeah, and your timing couldn't be better." He walked around the bed of the truck and tossed the end of another rope back to the guy. "Tie that down, would you? I know you're here to work on the ranch, but we've got a big deal happening at the fairgrounds today, and we could use all the hands we can get. You up for it?"

The guy shrugged as he secured the rope and tied a slip knot in the end of it. "Yeah, sure, I guess."

"Great. I need to grab something out of the barn.

Throw your gear in the house, and we'll get you settled later. The heads down the hall to the left if you need it."

"Okay."

The guy had a bit of a 'deer in the headlights' look to him as he pulled a leather duffle from the cab of his rig and headed toward the house, but Chevy didn't have time to dick around with directions and handholding. He was already running late, so not only would Gramps have his hide, but he knew Leni would be stressing too.

"Grab us a couple of bottles of water from the fridge on your way out," he called as he hurried toward the barn. Part of him wondered if he'd just made a colossal mistake sending some strange guy into the house, but Gramps had known Bucky Ferguson for years, and if Bucky vouched for the guy, Chevy doubted he'd steal their television and drive away. And so what if he did? A stolen tv was the least of his worries this morning. Besides, he and Dodge had been wanting a new flat screen anyway.

When he came out of the barn a few minutes later, the new guy was standing by Chevy's truck, two bottles of water clutched in his hands. "You good with dogs?" he asked, then told him to get in after he nodded.

The guy climbed in as Chevy whistled for Murphy and held the door for the golden to jump into the back of the king cab. "What's your name?" he finally thought to ask as he put the truck in gear and barreled down the drive and out onto the highway.

"Mack."

"Good to meet you, Mack. I'm Chevy. Not sure

what you've heard about the Lassiter boys, but I'll get it out of the way now. Yes, it's true, our mother named me and my brother's, Ford and Dodge, after the trucks that our different deadbeat dads drove away from us in. She was a real peace of work, that one. Then she dumped us on the doorstep of our grandparents when Dodge was barely able to walk, and we haven't seen her since. But she actually did us a favor, because Duke and June Lassiter were the best things that ever happened to us. Our grandma's gone now, but you'll meet Duke at the fairgrounds. That's our story. But maybe you'd already heard all that." He wasn't sure what Bucky, or his son, had told the guy. "So, what's yours?"

Mack grunted. "Too long to tell on the way into town."

"Fair enough." Chevy spent the rest of the ride filling him in on the details of the *Beans, Brews, and Bands* festival and how he could help them and the girls out that day.

Leni was standing in the driveway when they pulled up. She waved as Chevy hopped out and grabbed her around the waist, pulling her to him and capturing her mouth in a kiss.

"I've been thinking about doing that all morning," he told her when he finally pulled away.

She offered him a wry grin. "Were you also thinking about grabbing my butt? Because you've certainly got a firm grip on it."

"As a matter of fact…" he said, giving her ass a squeeze before letting her go. He gestured to the cowboy who had gotten out of the truck and was standing awkwardly in the yard. "This is Mack. He's the guy from Texas. He's gonna be helping us out today. Mack, this is my girl, Eleanor Gibbs. She's an aerospace engineer and works on rockets and spacecraft for a living."

"Cool," he said.

"Good to meet you," she told Mack, nodding his direction. "You can just call me, Leni. And that's my sister, Lorna." She pointed to her sister, who had Izzy's car seat looped over one arm as she wheeled herself out onto the porch with the knee scooter and was contemplating the railing.

Chevy moved toward her, but Mack was already ahead of him, taking the steps two at a time to reach Lorna.

"I got this," he said, gesturing to the knee scooter and offering her his elbow.

"Well, aren't you just the perfect gentleman?" she said, as she took his arm.

"Lorna, this is Mack," Chevy said, taking the car seat and smiling at Izzy as she gurgled and grinned up at him. "Hello sweet girl," he said to the baby, who had already stolen his heart.

Leni had already said hello to Murphy and finished packing the final totes in the spaces he'd left for her in the bed of the truck by the time he'd grabbed the base to Izzy's car seat and got her secured in the back seat.

They'd carted everything they could down to the fairgrounds the night before, and Maisie and Dodge had picked Max up earlier that morning and taken him out for pancakes to make it easier for Leni and Lorna to finish the final preparations for their booth.

Mack offered Lorna the front seat of the truck

and helped her into the cab then found a spot in the truck bed for the knee scooter before climbing into the backseat with Leni and Izzy.

"This is Isabel," Leni told Mack. "But we call her Izzy."

"Well, hello, Miss Izzy." He held his pinkie finger out and a grin creased his face as she wrapped her tiny hand around it.

"You've been here less than thirty minutes, and looks like you've already made a friend," Chevy said, winking at Leni as he ribbed Mack. Then he dropped the truck in gear and let out a whoop. "Who's ready to go eat some chili?"

Chapter Eighteen

Leni was already exhausted, and the day was only half over. Lorna and Elizabeth had been in charge of spooning up the samples of chili and passing out the judging sheets while Leni and Emily sold hundreds of water bottles.

Lorna was right. The blue and white water bottles were a huge hit. The crowd loved them.

It had been Leni's idea to send Emily over to the fairgrounds early, and she and one of her sister's had prefilled the first few hundred bottles with water, tea, or lemonade, leaving enough room at the top so all they had to do was put in a scoop of ice before handing it to the customer.

They'd enlisted Chevy and Mack's help when they'd run low, and two of them seemed to constantly be filling the water bottles while the other two were selling them.

The cookies were a hit as well, especially the homemade dog biscuits, but thankfully they had stayed up late the night before, and with Chevy's help had them all prepackaged and ready to go before they'd gone to bed.

With his charm and good-looks, Chevy was a natural born salesman, and he talked almost everyone who walked by their booth into buying either a water bottle or a cookie, and usually both. He'd also seemed to be getting along well with Mack, who seemed to fit right into the Lassiter clan, joking around with Dodge and Ford, and pitching in to help wherever he was needed, whether that was dishing up chili with Duke or helping Elizabeth make more lemonade.

Duke, Dodge, and Ford had mainly manned the Lassiter booth, helping the girls out if they needed something, while Chevy and Mack had seemed to run back and forth between the two. And from the comments they'd been hearing, their two chili recipes were among the favorites of the festival.

The Lassiter family's team name was *Chili Con Carnage*, and Duke had filled his chili with fresh vegetables and spices he'd grown on the ranch.

Lorna's recipe was more traditional, but Leni had added her own flair, and they both agreed that the recipe, even with the added sugar, was an amazing entry. Although Leni had wanted to name their team *Rocket Fuel*, Lorna had convinced her to keep *Red Hot Chili Preppers*, the name she'd used the year before. Leni had conceded, since the band had always been one of their favorites.

There were several other teams who were big contenders and giving them a run for their money. The two breweries were calling themselves *Netflix and Chili* and *Can't Handle the Heat*. A rowdy group of bull-riders and barrel racers, who were sampling more brews than beans, had dubbed themselves the *Roughstock Rumble*, the retirement home who had entered this year were *The Has-Beans,* the horse rescue ranch run by Bryn Callahan in Creedence, the next town over, deemed themselves *The Stew Crew,* and Carley Chapman, Lorna's hairdresser and friend, had put together a team with her hair salon, also in Creedence, called the *Spice Girls.*

The Presbyterians and their *Heavenly Heat* team were mainly trying to beat the scores of *Divine Delight,* the Baptists who'd been bragging about their chili recipe for months.

"Our biggest competition is the James boys from over in Creedence," Chevy told her. "Their team's name is *Never Been Hotter,* and they almost beat us last year."

All the kids from both Creedence and Woodland Hills attended the same high school, so Leni had known Rockford, Mason, and Colt James for years. "I should go over and say hi to those guys. I haven't seen them in years, but I do try to occasionally catch a hockey game if Rock is playing. Not that many of the guys I work with are totally into sports, but a few are quite impressed that I know a guy who plays for the NHL."

"Oh yeah, the Tipsy Pig fills up every time the Colorado Summit has a game, and we all turn out to cheer for our hometown hockey hero," Chevy said. "They're great guys. They've helped us out on the ranch before, and we've gone over to Creedence to help them. Their Aunt Sassy smokes a brisket that's fit for the angels—but this is chili we're talking about. So, today, the James boys are the enemy."

Leni laughed. "I think the library booths are so creative. They seem like they're getting a lot of votes." The two libraries from Woodland Hills and Creedence had set up together, and both had gone all out dressed like hobbits, dwarves, and elves for their teams, *The Lord of the Beans* and *the Fellowship of the Flame*. "And Maisie looks gorgeous dressed as Arwen Evenstar."

The librarian had also gone all out with a long silvery-blue gown covered by a gauzy white overlay and had braided strands of her hair and intertwined them through a silver elven crown that formed a point on her forehead and dripped with threads of tiny shimmering silver beads.

"They do look amazing, but I'm not that worried about them," Chevy told her. "Their chili is super tame, probably for all the kids, but I think they're getting more votes based on their Lembas Bread than their chili."

"I don't know. I had some of that Lembas bread," Leni said, referring to the thin cakes of leaf-wrapped elven bread the hobbits had eaten on their journey to Mordor. "It's delicious. Sort of like focaccia. And I took Max over earlier, and we both loved their chili recipe. It is tame, but it's good."

For all the stress of the day, Leni was still having a great time. It was fun to see so many people that she'd known when she was growing up in Woodland Hills, and she loved seeing the way her sister had blossomed and become part of the community.

And she *really* loved feeling like she was part of the Lassiter family again. She and Lorna had essentially grown up with Ford, Dodge, and Chevy. And their grandma, June, had been one of their Sunday school teachers. They both loved Duke with his easy laugh and his big bear hugs. All three of the boys were handsome and funny and just plain fun to be around. It made Leni feel special to be part of their world again.

The image of the acceptance letter of the job offer from NASA sitting in the top drawer of her dresser came to mind, but she put it out of her thoughts. Today was for family and friends, and she was determined to enjoy herself. She'd think about NASA tomorrow.

Or maybe the next day.

For now, she would tickle her adorable nephew, sip a microbrew, listen to great music, laugh with her sister, and enjoy the attention of the hot cowboy who had stolen her heart when she was fourteen years old.

The cold beer, hot chili, and feel-good bands had also been awesome. Strains of bluegrass and country songs filled the air throughout the afternoon, and several times, she caught herself tapping her foot or absently singing along to some of the more well-known lyrics.

Chevy had even talked her into stopping for a dance as they walked across the fairgrounds to get more ice from the freezers. It felt so good to be in his arms again, spinning and laughing and staring dreamily into his eyes as he whirled her around and held her in the crook of his shoulder.

It felt so good to be with him, period.

At times, she wanted to pinch herself, just to prove this wasn't a dream. She couldn't believe she was back in Woodland Hills, making out with Chevy Lassiter again, and having him introduce her as 'his girl'.

It also made Leni so happy to see her sister

laughing and having fun. And after the year she'd had, dealing with that snake, Lyle, and going through her pregnancy alone, all while raising a five-year-old boy, Lorna deserved to be happy.

A tendril of guilt wound its way around Leni's heart at being gone for so long and not spending enough time with her sister. Her job was so demanding, and so all-encompassing of her thoughts and brain-matter, that she had sometimes gone months without talking to Lorna or their mother.

It was easier when their mom was in town, and she knew the two of them were together and taking care of each other, but now that their mother had moved away, she imagined how alone Lorna must have felt. After she fell, the Lassiter clan had pitched in, and so had a few ladies from their church, but Leni noticed the absence of any real women friends.

"The few that I had deserted me after Lyle left, like cheating asshole husbands might be a disease they could catch," Lorna had told her one night when Leni had asked about her friends. "Or maybe they were worried that now that I was single, I would be on the prowl for their men. Which was hysterical. Because after that idiot, Lyle, left me, I turned into a hormonal single mom who was just trying to take care of her little boy, and was usually either sad, irritated, frustrated, bloated, or ragingly furious, with a huge belly, swollen ankles, and fighting back pain and hemorrhoids. The last thing I was interested in was flirting with their smelly husbands who drank too much and whose dad-bod bellies rivaled mine."

What she'd said had made sense, but Leni had still felt sad her sister had lost her female friends along with her husband, and the guilt had settled in her stomach like a stone falling to the bottom of a lake.

But she was here now. And that had to count for something.

She pledged to do something nice for her sister, treat her to a massage or buy her a gift card to a salon, or maybe pay her mortgage this month. Although Lorna had done so much for her over the years, that no amount of highlight appointments or back rubs could make up for. And her sister deserved to be treated to something. She was such a good person. And when she wasn't a raging hormonal pregnant woman whose husband had just walked out on her, she was almost always in a good mood.

Even with a broken ankle and an infant strapped to her chest, Lorna had been a trooper all day, passing out chili samples, cookies, and smiles.

Although, she hadn't had an infant strapped to her chest the whole time. She'd started out the day with Izzy in the baby carrier, then Leni and Chevy had each taken an hour or so with her, but it had surprised Leni that afternoon to see Mack also hawking water bottles with the baby strapped to his chest.

"I think Izzy is in love," Leni told her sister, nodding at the cowboy who was grinning down at the baby who had a hold of his pinkie again.

"She's not the only one," Lorna said. "Who is this guy? And how do I get him to carry me around all day?"

Leni laughed and bumped her sister's hip. "Why do you need a cowboy to carry you around when you've got Betty?"

"Ha. Yeah, like Betty the wonder-scooter is a perfect

substitute for a six-foot-something hot cowboy with big muscles and a killer grin."

"Fair point," Leni said, laughing again and thinking that was about the same way she described Chevy. Now that she thought about it, Mack kind of reminded her of Chevy, with his dark hair, blue eyes, good sense of humor, and kind temperament. She hoped those last few qualities would help him to be an asset to the ranch and he would work out and be able to help the Lassiter men.

Chevy interrupted them as he hurried back to their booth, a concerned look on his face. "Apparently, there's been a sleeper team this year that might be pulling ahead of us. Aunt Sassy put a team together called *Chili Chili Bang Bang*, and I'm hearing their recipe is getting rave reviews."

"I heard they're passing out tiny wine slushies with their samples," Lorna said.

"I think my family is doing pretty well this year, too," Emily told them. Her ginger-haired family had dubbed themselves the *Grateful Red,* and their chili was full of carrots and red peppers.

"Step it up, team," Chevy called out to both booths. "Sell more cookies. Pet more dogs. One of us has to win this thing."

Chapter Nineteen

IN THE END, neither of their teams won first place.

The Lassiter's had taken second though.

Leni and her sister had pulled in a solid fourth spot, which still earned a ribbon and a plaque and made Lorna happy, since she could display it at the shop.

The Chili Dawgs, a new team formed by the family who ran the local hardware store had come in strong with chunks of smoked sausage, brats, and bacon in their recipe, and they nabbed the winning trophy and bragging rights for the year. They'd been cooking the meat all day on the new smokers they were selling at the store, and the consensus from the Lassiter clan was that the scent of smoked sausage and the extra samples of brats in the barbeque sauce that they *also* sold in their store, was the catalyst to their win.

"That was some damn good chili though," Chevy said as they washed up the last of the dishes that night.

They'd already put Max to bed and Chevy, Mack, Leni and her sister were all in the kitchen of Lorna's house. Lorna had finished nursing and put Izzy down and was trying to wheel the knee-scooter around the kitchen to help with the dishes but kept bumping into the cabinets and everyone else's legs.

Leni finally gave her a job that required her to sit at the kitchen table with Mack while she and Chevy finished washing out the last of the five-gallon buckets and all the coolers.

"Welcome to the family," Lorna told Mack. "What an introduction. Talk about getting thrown into the deep end to learn how to swim. That was a lot for your first day here."

Mack offered her a shrug. "I thought it was fun."

"You must have a lot of siblings the way you were able to just jump right into the mix," Leni said, pulling out a chair and sitting down next to her sister.

Mack shook his head. "Not really. I was raised as an only child."

"That sounds tough," Chevy said, setting four glasses of ice water on the table before dropping into the chair next to Leni. "We give each other a hard time, but I don't know what I'd do without my brothers."

"You're lucky," Mack said, taking a glass then passing one to Lorna. "You need anything else?" he asked her.

"Yes," she said. "A million dollars, a great night's sleep, and a weekend in Paris."

He chuckled as he took out his wallet and looked inside. "No million dollars or a trip to Paris, but I could offer you a Subway card that's only two stamps away from a free sub."

She held out her hand for the card. "That's the best offer I've had all year. I'll take it."

He started to hand her the card then pulled it back.

"How about I get the last two stamps by picking up sandwiches for you and your sister some night next week, and *then* I'll give you the card and the free sub is yours."

"Deal," Lorna said with a laugh.

"Great. How about Monday night?"

"Perfect."

He pulled out his phone. "I'd better get your number so I can text you for your sub order."

Chevy chuckled as he muttered, "Smooth, bro," not quite under his breath.

Leni laughed. "Works out well for me too, since I'm now also getting a free sub out of this deal. Although I should be treating you guys to a meal for all the help you gave us today. Seriously, I don't know what we would have done without you."

"Yes, thanks so much," Lorna added, lifting her glass for a toast. "Here's to good food and good times, to new friends…" She glanced first over at Mack then turned to Leni and Chevy. "…and old friends becoming new ones again."

"I'll drink to that," Chevy said, as they all clinked their glasses together. "And speaking of new friends, Mack and I should get back to the ranch. Duke will want to get you settled in proper, and I've still got chores to do."

Two days later, Leni pulled her car into the Lassiter ranch, happy to see Chevy's pickup parked in front of the house.

She had worked at the coffee shop the day before,

then she and Lorna had spent most of the afternoon recuperating from the festival, napping with Izzy and watching movies with Max. Chevy had dropped by with a couple of pizzas and sworn that he'd just been thinking about how much he'd wanted to see the latest Minion movie. Leni had been impressed that he'd stayed awake through the whole thing.

She'd been even more impressed when he'd offered to put Max to bed while she straightened the kitchen and helped Lorna with Izzy.

Something that had felt a lot like love had come over her when she came up the stairs and heard him telling her nephew what happens when you give a mouse a cookie. The sweet giggles of the five-year-old made her heart want to burst.

She'd stood in the hall outside of Max's room wondering if she really was in love with Chevy Lassiter again. Or if she'd ever stopped loving him in the first place.

Then he'd come out and asked her if she knew what would happen if you gave a cowboy an aerospace engineer, and she stopped thinking altogether as he carried her into her bedroom and shut the door.

It was Monday morning now, and the coffee shop was closed, so Leni had picked up donuts and decided to surprise Chevy and his brothers with them.

She pulled up next to Chevy's truck and did a quick lip gloss refresh in the visor mirror, swiping on a new layer of the minty soft pink shimmer. She'd taken a little extra time with her makeup that morning and set her hair in hot curlers to get the bouncy waves that he liked.

Digging through the pile of new summer things

she'd bought when she realized she was staying in Woodland Hills longer than she'd planned, she found a white top with tiny flutter sleeves and a little black skirt that showed off the tan she'd gotten since she'd been here and started spending more time outside in the sun instead of inside at her computer.

Under the skirt, she'd put on a pair of black thong panties, not exactly *planning* to seduce him somewhere on the ranch this morning, but hey, if a hayloft proved available…there was a strong possibility she might haul him into it.

She grabbed the pastry box and met Dodge on the porch as she was walking up to the house. "Hey Dodge. I brought some donuts out to say thank you for all the help you guys gave us at the festival on Saturday."

"That was nothing. We all had fun." He held his hand out for the bakery box. "But there's not a Lassiter here that would ever turn down a donut."

She handed him the box. "Chevy around?"

He nodded absently as he opened the lid and considered his donut choices. "Yeah, I think he just got back. He's been out with Jolene all morning. She was causing drama—probably jealous of all the time you two have been spending together."

Leni's heart stopped, and bile rose in her throat. "Wait. Did you say *Jolene*? She's here? Now? *With* Chevy?"

He'd said he wasn't seeing anyone.

He lied.

How could she have been so stupid?

I trusted him.

She pressed her lips together to keep a sob from escaping.

He's gonna break my heart all over again.

"Yeah. I think they just got back from a ride. He's out in the barn with her—"

But she didn't hear the rest of what he said as she turned around and stomped toward the barn.

She threw open the door, anxiety filling her chest as she prepared herself to catch the man she'd thought she loved in the arms of the same woman he'd left her for all those years ago.

She marched through the alley of the barn but found Chevy alone standing outside one of the stalls watering and brushing a brown horse.

His face lit as he looked up and saw her. "Leni. Hey. What are you doing here?" He took a step toward her, but she held her hand up like she was warding off a vampire with a wooden stake and a strand of garlic.

"Never mind that. What are *you* doing here?" she asked with barely controlled fury in her voice. She could feel heat burning her cheeks.

He stared at her, a confused expression on his face. "Um, I don't know what you mean. I'm just brushing my horse. Everything okay?"

"No. *Nothing's* okay. I can't believe I fell for this again. Fell for *you*." She spat the words at him, the anger and humiliation building inside her. "You are such a freaking liar."

He took a step back like she'd physically slapped him. "What are you talking about?"

Leni glanced around the barn. "Where is she?"

"She who?"

"Don't play dumb with me. You said you weren't

seeing anyone, that you didn't have a girlfriend. Yet, within a week of us getting back together, which, by the way, is *over* now, you're back with your old girlfriend."

"Leni, please. Slow down. I don't know what you heard, but I *don't* have a girlfriend. And I seriously have no idea what you're talking about."

"Stop lying!" she screamed at him, hot tears pricking her eyes. "Dodge already told me you were out here with *her*. He said you just got back from a ride *with Jolene*."

The horse let out a whinny and stomped her foot.

Chevy's eyes widened, and he breathed out one word. "Oh."

Before he could answer, Ford walked into the barn. He stopped when he got to them, and his gaze went back-and-forth between Chevy and Leni and then landed on his brother. "Am I interrupting something?"

"Oh no," Leni spat, still fuming as she planted one fist on her hip. "Chevy was just about to introduce me to *Jolene*."

"Oh yeah? That's great. I'm surprised you haven't met her before." Ford crossed behind Chevy to give the horse he'd been brushing a pat on the neck. "She's a great girl. Aren't you, Jolene?"

Leni sucked in a breath, and her stomach churned. She bent forward and grabbed her knees, afraid that she might vomit.

"Whoa. You okay?" Ford asked, taking a step forward, but Chevy reached out to hold him back.

She stood back up, but pressed a hand to her chest, pushing against it like she was trying to hold her heart inside, as if the shattered pieces might ooze out between her fingers.

"*Jolene?*" she said, her voice coming out in a whisper. "*That's* Jolene? That *horse?*"

"Yeah," Ford said, clearly confused as he rubbed her neck again. "Isn't she a beauty?"

She swallowed, anger taking the place of the nauseous feeling that had her stomach roiling. "Just *when* did Chevy acquire this beautiful horse?"

Chevy stood stock still, his face as green as her stomach felt.

Ford shrugged. "I don't know. About ten years ago, I guess." He turned to Chevy. "You got her towards the end of that summer you graduated high school, wasn't it?"

Chevy looked at Leni, not answering his brother out loud, but slowly nodded his head.

Every emotion was tearing through Leni—sadness, nausea, disbelief, fury. The tears she'd been holding back finally broke as she sobbed out, "A horse? You broke up with me—broke my heart into a million pieces—for *a horse?*"

"Leni." His voice was pleading as Chevy took a tentative step toward her.

But she held up her hand as she took a step back. "No. Don't."

She pressed her fingers to her lips, trying to hold back more sobs as she turned and ran out of the barn.

Chapter Twenty

CHEVY FELT LIKE he was going to puke. He knew having Leni Gibbs back in his life was too good to be true.

"What in the Sam hell just happened?" Ford asked, the expression on his face showing the shock that Chevy felt.

"I think what happened is that Leni just broke up with me."

"What? Why? And what the hell does she have against Jolene?"

Chevy scrubbed his hand over his face, suddenly weary to his bones. "You remember how I pushed her away that summer when she got into MIT? Broke up with her? Told her I didn't love her anymore?"

Ford winced. "Yeah, I remember."

"Well, I was having a hard time getting her to believe me, so I told her I'd fallen in love with someone else. Someone who needed me more and deserved all my attention. And I told her it was Jolene."

"Ah. And I'm assuming that from Leni's reaction, you failed to mention that Jolene was a horse. Or I guess, at the time, a foal."

Chevy nodded. "Yep."

Ford shook his head. "Wow. You are a total dumbass."

"Yep."

"So, what the hell are you doing standing here? Why aren't you going after her?"

"Did you see how mad she was? She probably won't ever talk to me again."

"She won't if you don't go after her."

"Don't you think I should at least let her cool off?"

"No. I do not," Ford said. "Not if you want to have any chance of saving this relationship."

"Right." He looked at Jolene.

"I'll finish brushing her and put her away," Ford said.

Chevy patted his pockets. Shit. His truck keys were in the house. "Thanks brother."

"Just go."

Leni had cried the whole way back to her house—big gulping sobs—in between screaming in frustration and then dissolving into tears again.

For ten years, she'd believed that Chevy had found someone else to love—someone better than her. And all this time, that someone had been a damn horse.

She pulled into the driveway and turned off the car. Grabbing a handful of napkins from the center console, she wiped the tears from her face and the snot from her nose. Not that it would do any good. Her sister would still know she'd been crying.

How could she not? One glance in the rearview mirror showed her puffy swollen eyes and red cheeks.

She tossed the napkins to the floor of her car, got out, and slammed the door. Hurrying up the porch steps, she almost collided with Duke as he was coming out of the house.

"Whoa there, darlin'," he said, wrapping her in his arms. "What's happened?"

"Your grandson happened," she wailed as the tears started to fall again.

"Aw hell," he muttered as he hugged her tight. "Just let it out."

Her shoulders shook as she sobbed into his.

"You wanna talk about it," Duke asked when she'd finally cried herself out. He pulled what she hoped was a clean handkerchief from his pocket and handed it to her as she sank onto the top porch step. "Lorna's not here. I just ran into her as I was coming up to drop off a pan of homemade macaroni and cheese. She told me Elizabeth was picking her and the kids up, and they were going to lunch and to do some shopping before heading to the library to see Maisie for story hour. She said they were going to be gone most of the afternoon and asked me to put the mac and cheese in the fridge. I'm sorry you just missed her." He lifted one shoulder in a shrug. "But I'm a good listener if you want to share your troubles."

Her shoulders drooped. "Even if my troubles are the fault of your stupid grandson?"

He nodded. "Especially then."

She wiped her nose with the handkerchief then balled it into her fist as she told him what happened. "I've harbored the worst feelings to this horrible boyfriend-stealing Jolene, and all this time, she was just a horse."

"To be fair, she's a pretty good horse. And she's probably what saved Chevy that first year after you left."

"Saved him from what?"

"From dying of a broken heart. Gosh, he was a mess that summer." He tipped her chin up to look at him. "That boy loved you. Still does, I believe. Loved you so much that he let you go."

She huffed. "Loved me so much that he had to fake a relationship *with a horse* just to get away from me."

"He wasn't trying to get away from you, honey." Duke's tone softened. "He was trying to let you get away *from him*. You have to understand. Those boys, all three of them, were deserted not just by their no-good fathers, but their own mother, too. She's my daughter, and I'll always love her, but I'm still disappointed in the way she so callously abandoned her sons. She did something to each of them—broke them in a way only a mother could. But know this— Chevy didn't break up with you. He let you go."

"Why? I loved him. I would have stayed with him forever."

"But that's exactly why. He couldn't let you do that. From the way he tells it, you didn't listen when he told you to go to that fancy college and leave him behind, so he had to take drastic measures. And apparently Jolene was the measure he landed on."

The roar of an engine had them both looking up as Chevy's truck came barreling down the street and screeched to a halt in front of the house. He was out of the door and crossing the lawn before the engine barely had time to stop.

"Gramps," Chevy said, apparently not losing all his senses as he nodded his head to his grandfather.

"About time you got here, son," Duke told him, dropping a hand on his grandson's shoulder and giving it a squeeze. "I'll git out of here and let you two talk." He gave Leni a one-armed hug, leaning in to whisper, "Remember what I said."

She and Chevy didn't say anything as they watched Duke amble toward his pickup and drive away.

Then she turned to Chevy. "I'm so mad at you. I'm not sure I'm ready to hear anything you have to say." She left him standing on the porch and walked into the house.

He followed her inside and shut the door behind him. "Then you need to get ready, because I have plenty to tell you."

She started to open the door again, but he reached over her head to push it shut, fencing her in between him and the back of the door. "Please Leni, just listen to me," he pleaded as he looked down at her.

She was caged between him and the door, but not in a scary way. He would never hurt her. She didn't feel threatened, but being this close to him, the scent of him surrounding her, already had her defenses faltering. She crossed her arms over her chest and jutted out a hip to show her defiance. "I'm listening."

He leaned his head down, slowly, deliberately, until his forehead touched hers. "First of all, I'm sorry, Leni. I'm so damn sorry. I never meant to hurt you." He let out a breath. "Well, I guess that's not true. I did mean to hurt you. I wanted you to hate me."

"Why?"

"Because you had to hate me if I was ever gonna get you to leave."

"You bastard. You pushed me away, broke my heart and ruined me for any other man, and for ten years, you made me believe that you met someone else, and that she was better than I was. That I wasn't good enough, pretty enough, or sweet enough for a guy like you."

"Good lord, Leni, you were too good, too pretty, *too everything* for a guy like me."

"So, what then? You just didn't love me enough to stay with me?"

He sighed. "I loved you *too* much. If I had my way, I would have stayed with you forever. But that wouldn't have been fair to you."

"You think it was *fair* to tell me you didn't love me anymore and that you'd found someone else who needed you more?"

"No, of course not. Although, to be honest, Jolene really did need me. Her mama died giving birth to her, and I bottle-fed her for months."

She narrowed her eyes at him. "Are you really trying to argue that I should be feeling sorry for that horse right now?"

He huffed out a small laugh. "No. I'm not trying to argue at all. I'm trying to tell you that I was an idiot. And I'm sorry. I was a kid, a teenage boy, who was in love with the smartest girl in the school, the smartest person he'd ever met. A girl who'd dreamed of space and building rockets and was so damn brilliant that she was offered a scholarship to one of the best schools in the nation and had a chance to leave me and this small town and make those dreams of hers come true. I knew, even then, that I never deserved you. I got to love you, for a little while, and I loved you with everything I had, but I always knew that I wasn't the kind of guy who got to have someone like you. I wasn't the kind of guy worth giving up a stick of gum for, let alone lifelong dreams that you had a real shot of turning into a reality. And I sure as hell wasn't gonna let you give up everything for me."

"So, you broke up with me for your horse?" Her tone was still annoyed, but his words had touched her heart.

"No, I broke up with you for *you*. So you could have all those things you always dreamed of."

She reached up to touch his cheek. He was so sweet, so damn handsome. How could he ever think he didn't deserve to be loved? "Oh Chevy, how could you ever think you weren't worth staying for?"

His voice was quiet as he answered, "Because nobody has ever stayed for me before."

His words hit her straight in the heart.

She knew the feeling. That was why it was so hard for her to trust a man. Not one of them had ever stuck around—not her father and not the first boy she gave her heart to. Which was why she had chosen to never give it away again.

He let out a heavy breath as he scrubbed a hand over his cheek. "It's just a hell of a lot easier to push people away *before* they have a chance to walk out on you."

"But you didn't even give me the choice, or the chance, to stay."

"I know. Because you might have stayed. For a

while. You might have given it all up and stayed here. With me. But eventually, you would have regretted that decision, resented me, and left anyway. So, it was easier to push you away, to make you think I didn't love you anymore, to make you leave." He closed his eyes and pulled in a breath. "I take that back. It wasn't *easier*. Pushing you away was the hardest thing I've ever had to do."

He reached up to cup her cheek in his palm. "But I would do it again. In a heartbeat. I would sacrifice everything, if it meant giving you a chance to make your dreams come true."

"That's so unfair."

"Is it? Why? You left. You went to that fancy school. You're doing the things you always dreamed of. That makes it worth it."

Her sister, Duke, and now Chevy himself, were all telling her that the reason he broke up with her was *for* her. To give her a chance to follow her dreams. How could she hate him for that?

"I hate that something I did made you cry," he said, rubbing her cheek with his thumb. "I should have told you about Jolene sooner. I'm sorry that it made you so upset."

Finding out that Jolene was a horse was a blow, but her reaction to it, the soul-wracking sobs, was about more than just Chevy's deception all those years ago.

She peered up at him, at the blue eyes she'd looked into so many times. "I think I was upset about more than just the horse. This whole thing, being back here with you again, has brought up a lot of feelings, and I think some of that came out in my reaction.

What happened with us changed me, and I've spent a decade building this fortress around my heart...brick by brick...keeping people at a distance. Especially men. And then I came back here and in less than a week, I'm back in your life, and in your bed, and those bricks felt like they were starting to crumble. But then I found out this big thing that I've believed for so long, that has formed parts of my identity, was just this weird false lie, and all those walls shot up again. I didn't know what to do with all those feelings. Except let them out in anger and tears."

"Sometimes it helps to get it out instead of keeping all that bottled up inside. But I feel awful bad that some stupid idea I had when I was practically a kid changed how you felt about yourself. That was never my intention. I wanted you to fly, to go into the world and realize how amazing and smart you were and to be so successful and happy that you never looked back."

She offered him a rueful smile. "I did do some of that."

"I'm glad. And I'm really glad you came back to Woodland Hills and that you gave me a chance to show you how much I still care about you. I don't want those walls up between us anymore."

"I've spent years protecting myself with them. You can't just tear the whole thing down with one amazing afternoon at a cabin."

His face broke into a slow smile, and he tilted his head, offering her a huge heaping helping of that Chevy Lassiter charm. "We could always go back up and try to see if a *second* amazing afternoon at a cabin would work any better…"

The rest of her anger slipped away as a smile tugged at the corners of her lips. "You're an idiot."

"Yeah, I am. I'm an idiot for ever letting you believe you weren't enough." His teasing charm was gone as his gaze bore into her with a new intensity. "I have *never* stopped thinking about you. I still can't believe I get to hold you again." He took a step forward, pushing her back against the door as he leaned in to brush his lips against her neck. His warm breath on her skin sent a shiver down her spine, and she swallowed. "To touch you again…" he continued as he ran his fingers lightly up her arm, across her shoulder and up the side of her jaw. He lifted her chin and grazed the edge of his thumb over her bottom lip. "…to kiss you again."

She sucked in a breath, heat and yearning surging through her body as he moved his mouth closer to hers, the scruff on his cheeks scraping the edge of hers, then his lips skimmed over hers, just the barest touch, enough to make them tingle with anticipation seconds before he captured her mouth in a hungry kiss.

The kiss was deep and demanding, and she tilted her head as she invited him deeper.

Her arms went around his neck, and a soft whimper escaped her as she kissed him back, hard, with a fierce passion as she lost herself in the essence of him.

His body was pressed against hers, and she could feel how much he wanted her. His hand was in her hair, and he cupped the back of her neck, holding her in place as he feasted on her lips. His kisses shifted from her mouth to her neck to that spot just below her ear.

His voice was husky as he spoke into her ear. "If your family wasn't here, I swear I'd take you against this door right now."

Chapter Twenty-One

All her normal logic and reason left Leni as she was consumed with wanting this man. "My family *isn't* here," she said, in between another kiss. "Elizabeth took them out to lunch. We're alone."

A growl emanated from the back of his throat as his hand slid down her side, over her hip, and cupped her ass. His kisses grew hotter, hungrier, as he ravaged her mouth, her neck, her breasts—demanding surrender but promising pleasure.

Then he had her wrists captured in one hand, her arms held over her head and flat against the door, as his other hand slipped under her skirt and pushed aside the thin strap of her thong panties.

This wasn't exactly the hayloft she'd imagined, but it was still hot as hell.

Panting his name, she tipped her head back, her shoulders meeting the resistance of the door, powerless against this man, her thoughts only on the bliss of his lips on her neck and his hand between her legs. Stroking, caressing, pulling at the need and desire building inside her.

Her whole body surrendered to him, every part

wanting and aching for his touch, desire coursing through her like the flames of a wildfire.

This felt out of control—and Leni was all about control—but at this moment, with her back against the door, her nipples tight and aching, and Chevy's hand under her skirt, she didn't care. All she cared about was the feel of this man against her and the swirl of heat building at her center—a swirl that had her crying out as she writhed against the tantalizing friction—frantic for release as he stroked and rubbed and then…yes…yes…now…she succumbed to the pleasure as the sensations rocketed through her.

She sagged against him, trying to catch her breath, a little in shock at the frenzied heat and reckless abandon of what had just happened.

Chevy leaned his forehead against hers, a little out of breath himself. "That was so damn…"

"Hot," she finished for him.

"Yeah. And now I just want to get you in a bed and under me."

Feeling brazen and sexy, she grinned up at him. "Race you upstairs."

She kicked off her sandals and ran for the stairs, shrieking in laughter as he caught her and scooped her into his arms to carry her up and into her room, pausing halfway up and again in the hallway to kiss her before setting her on her bed.

She scooted back against the headboard, flushed with heat, watching as he practically tore off his T-shirt, the perfection of his body making her want to weep, and she couldn't wait to touch and explore every hard muscled inch of it.

He kicked off his boots and shucked down his

jeans, then he was in the bed, the weight of his body on top of her as his lips found hers.

He stopped kissing her only long enough to pull her top over her head and free her of her bra. She wrapped herself around him, desperate to regain everything she'd missed over the last ten years.

She loved the way he looked at her, his eyes hooded, hungry for her. Scorching need coursed through her again as he lavished her breasts with attention, kneading and kissing and sampling their tender tips.

Then his weight was on her again, his breath warm against her ear, his hard body flush against hers, his strong hands gripping her, and everything else fell away. Everything except the feel of this man, the one who had captured her heart all those years ago, and never quite let it go.

She'd spent years trying to forget him, but occasionally, in the middle of the night, in the lonely, dark shadows of her bedroom, she let herself think about him, let herself imagine what he was doing now, and dream about what would have happened if they would have stayed together.

Would their sweet babies have had his dark hair and blue eyes? Would they have spent weekends at the cabin, fishing and hiking and making love under the mountain stars? Would they have gotten married at the ranch like they'd talked about and ridden off in a horse-drawn carriage?

It hurt enough to think about the future they would never have, but sometimes, especially if she'd had a glass of wine, *or three*, she let herself imagine times like this, with her and Chevy naked in her bed, kissing, touching, caressing. If she could close her eyes, she could remember the feather soft feel of his fingers skimming down her arm before taking her hand.

But this wasn't a memory. This was happening, and it was heat and heedless need, and her body hummed with tension as the sensations ricocheted through her.

Her short skirt was stretchy cotton, and where he'd earlier pushed it up to her waist, he now pulled it and the tiny panties down her legs and tossed them on the floor.

The fantasies she'd had of them before couldn't touch the reality of the way they were now, the added broadness of his shoulders, the new strength—and tenderness—of his hands, the rough scrape of his whiskers on the tender parts of her inner thigh, and—lord have mercy—the new things he knew how to do with his tongue.

Oh, the things that man could do with his tongue. Those were what would now fill her middle of the night fantasies.

She leaned across the bed, yanked open the drawer of her nightstand, and tossed the new box of condoms she'd purchased toward Chevy. He caught them in one hand and tore the box open, ripping the cardboard and sending foil packets scattering across the bed and hitting the floor. He nabbed one from between the folds of the sheets, tore it open and covered himself.

Then he was nudging her thighs apart, taking his place between them, and she wrapped her legs around him, acutely aware of every sensation, as they fell into a rhythm—both familiar and new.

A growl hummed in Chevy's throat as he leaned

down to capture her lips. But he didn't just kiss her, he stole her breath with his desire.

Her body responded, clinging to him as if she were drowning, and he was the only thing that could save her.

"You're mine," he said, his voice husky and breathless against her neck, claiming her as the rough scrape of his whiskers grazed her skin.

He moved with her, slow at first then faster, rocking her body with need. She took what he offered and demanded more. Shimmers of heat flooded through her, and she thought she might die from the feeling of pure pleasure pooling in the ache between her legs.

He let out a moan as his restraint slipped, his fingers digging into her hips, his teeth grazing her shoulder. She clutched his back, savoring the sweet torment as he drove her higher and higher. Then she was falling, crying out and giving herself to the exquisite sensations that rolled through her.

He kissed her, catching her cries in his mouth, his strong arms holding her close as his muscles tightened and a low growl hummed against her lips, rocking with her as he matched her release.

Spent, he collapsed on the bed, pulling her to him as he pressed his lips to the side of her head. She lay next to him, emotions rolling through her as she tried to catch her breath.

She was all about logic, and yet, everything about this time with Chevy was *illogical*. It didn't make sense how hard she'd fallen again in such a short time and how deep her feelings already were, but it was real.

They lay together, their breath evening out, the

drowsy feeling of great sex washing over her. But this wasn't just sex, they'd crossed into something new, something different than the fevered fumbling of two teenagers.

This was trust, this was handing over control of herself to this man, the one who'd shattered her heart, and taking a leap of faith that he wouldn't destroy her again.

Chevy stirred beside her. "Hey," he said, his voice sleepy and soft. "I have a question to ask, and it's an important one."

She braced herself for another onslaught of emotions. "Okay, ask me anything."

"Any chance there's some of those cookies you made this weekend left?"

She sat up, joy filling that empty place that had been inside her, then laughed as she whacked him with a pillow.

Chapter Twenty-Two

THE FLAVORS OF chocolate and butterscotch blended on Leni's tongue as Chevy fed her another bite, and she swore no cookie had never tasted so good.

They'd gotten dressed, just in case Lorna and the kids came home early, and she was sitting on the kitchen counter, the tall cowboy nestled between her legs as he stole kisses from her in between bites of cookie.

His mouth tasted like vanilla and sugar, and she wanted to kiss him forever.

Forever?

That thought caught her by surprise.

What did kissing Chevy *forever* look like?

It would mean staying in Woodland Hills. His family, the ranch, were here—there was no way he'd leave them.

But could she really come back here? For good?

She had a life in Washington, an apartment, three plants, her favorite Thai food takeout place.

And what about her job?

What about NASA?

Chevy's brow furrowed as he looked at something out the window behind her. "Did you know you have a cow in your backyard?"

"What?" She whipped her head around, all thoughts of her rhododendron and chicken Pad Thai forgotten, to see a reddish-brown cow chewing its cud while standing in her sister's flowerbed.

"Is it yours?"

"Lorna hasn't even let Max get a dog yet. You think she'd have a pet cow?"

Chevy held up his hands. "Hey, this could be some newfangled hipster thing your sister is doing to save the environment by not using a lawn mower."

She playfully punched him in the shoulder. "That's *not* our cow. And I think my sister would take offense at being called a newfangled hipster."

"She has a jar of that kombucha crap in her fridge, sells fancy seven-dollar coffee drinks, and has avocado toast on the menu in a coffee shop in the middle of the mountains."

"Touche." Leni let out a groan as the cow pulled up one of her sister's gorgeous geraniums. "Not the geraniums," she called out as she knocked on the window. "Lorna just planted those this summer. Why can't it be eating the dandelions?"

"I love that your concern is more about which flowers it's eating than over why you have a cow that doesn't belong to you standing in your yard."

"What should we do?"

"Figure out who it belongs to and take it back."

"I solve complex problems in my job that can involve aerodynamic fluid flow or propulsion and combustion, but nothing in my skill set has prepared me to solve either of those options."

He chuckled. "Then it's a good thing your boyfriend is a cowboy who runs a cattle ranch. I consider myself fairly proficient in all things heifer related."

She offered him a side-eye. "Are you including *me* in that proficiency?"

He let loose a belly laugh as he lifted her off the counter and set her on her feet. "I wouldn't dare."

"Not if you wanted to live to see tomorrow."

"Why don't we start by seeing if she's carrying a brand. That might tell us what ranch she's from."

"How do you know it's a *she*?"

He raised an eyebrow. "Remember that heifer proficiency we were just talking about? You stick to rockets—let me manage the bovine."

Gladly. Besides, she was still thinking about how easily he'd thrown out the word *boyfriend* a few seconds ago.

Her phone buzzed as she followed him through the door. She pulled it from the front pocket of her shorts and saw her sister's name as she tapped the screen. "Sorry Sis, I can't talk right now. There's a strange cow in our backyard."

Lorna gasped. But apparently not for the reason Leni thought she would. *Not* because she'd told her a cow was in her yard. "I *just* saw on Nextdoor this morning that someone was missing a cow. Is it reddish brown with a white spot in the middle of its forehead that's shaped like the state of South Dakota?"

Leni blinked, not able to keep up with all the craziness in her sister's comments. "South Dakota? You know I'm terrible at geography. And I'm not close enough to the cow to see what state appears to be on his forehead."

"South Dakota is the one that's like a rectangle except the bottom right corner is broken so it looks like some of the Dakota is spilling out."

"Thank you for that social studies lesson. What do you mean you saw it on Nextdoor?"

"You know, it's like the app for people to stay in touch with what's happening in their neighborhoods."

"I know *what* Nextdoor is. But I thought people usually posted about their missing dogs or lost cats or to get a recommendation for a good plumber."

"Well, apparently in Woodland Hills, people also use it to post about their missing heifers."

Leni laughed as she put her sister on speaker. "It's Lorna. She said someone posted on Nextdoor that they were missing a cow."

He reached for his phone. "Oh nice. I'll pull up the app."

"Don't bother," Lorna told him. "I already did. It looks like the cow belongs to Berniece Buckley. *If* it's the one with South Dakota on its forehead."

Leni shook her head. "Is there *more than one* missing cow on the app?" she asked her sister as Chevy mouthed 'South Dakota?' at her.

"Hmm," Lorna said, sounding distracted as if she were scrolling through her phone. "Not today."

"Phew. Well, that's sure a stroke of luck," Leni said, not even trying to disguise the sarcasm in her voice. She pointed to the white spot on the cow's forehead. "Does that look like South Dakota to you?"

He squinted at the spot. "Yeah. I can see that."

"Yay." Lorna's cheer came through the speaker." This says her name is Babydoll, and she loves carrots, dandelions, and molasses."

And apparently geraniums.

Leni turned to Chevy. "So can you watch her while I go whip up a batch of carrot pancakes covered in molasses?"

Chevy ignored her as he got closer and crooned to the cow. "Hey Babydoll. You ready to go home?"

The cow took a few steps toward him then nuzzled her head into his shoulder.

"I've got some carrots in the fridge you can use. Do you think you can you catch her?" Lorna asked. She was really invested in this cow thing.

"We don't have to. She's currently cuddling into Chevy's shoulder. He just said her name, and she's practically crawling into his lap. I swear that man's charm knows no bounds."

"Aww. That's so sweet. Take a picture," her sister instructed through her laughter.

Leni lifted her phone and snapped a picture of the cow cuddling up to the cowboy. Then she flipped the phone screen and got a couple of selfies of the same shot but with her in the foreground.

She made a mental note to make sure she got another selfie of just the two of them. She didn't really want the only current pic she had of her and Chevy to have a heifer in it.

Lorna laughed harder when Leni sent her the picture of Chevy and one of the selfies with her making a goofy face. "Max, look at this picture of Aunt Leni with a cow in our backyard."

Max's excited voice came through the phone

speaker. "There's a cow in our backyard? Can we keep it?"

Lorna laughed harder. "No. We can't keep it. It belongs to a lady named Berniece, and she's missing it. Aunt Leni and Chevy are going to take it home."

"How are they going to do that?" Max asked.

Good question, kid.

"Hey Chevy, how *are* we going to get this cow home?" she asked after she'd hung up with her sister.

"Seems like we have a couple of choices. I know the Buckley place. It's probably a fifteen-minute walk if we go back through the woods and cut through downtown. Which is how I'm assuming she got here. Or I can go back to the ranch and hook up a trailer to take her home in. Probably take me thirty or forty minutes."

"The trailer sounds like the easier way to transport a cow, but if we can get her home in half the time, it makes more sense just to walk her back. I'm sure Miss Berniece is probably worried."

"I agree. I think I've got a halter and a lead rope in my truck. And I might even have some alfalfa cubes—our cows love those. You keep an eye on her while I grab some stuff."

"What do I do if she tries to leave?"

Chevy looked at the cow peacefully munching on another geranium. "I don't think you have to worry, but just holler at me if you get into trouble."

"Lorna said she had some carrots in the fridge. Grab those on your way back through. And my purse too. It's the little black cross-body bag sitting on the kitchen table. It's got my wallet in it."

"You gonna try to bribe the cow to walk home?"

"Ha. Not with what's in my wallet. I never have cash. I just want my sunglasses and my lip gloss."

He raised an eyebrow.

"Hey, a girl wants to look her best when she's walking a cow through the center of town."

Ten minutes later, they had made it through the wooded area behind the house and were cutting through downtown. Chevy had easily coaxed the halter on Babydoll then clipped the lead rope to it.

Thanks to a mixture of carrots, alfalfa cubes, and a few more of Lorna's geraniums, they had lured the cow through the woods. But now she was just following along behind them as they walked in the bike lane of Main Street.

They had to look hysterical—just a normal Monday afternoon and a nice couple taking their cow for a walk downtown.

Lots of people waved and several stopped to say hello to Babydoll and mention that they'd seen the Nextdoor post and had been on the lookout for her.

Leni and Chevy also got several looks, especially since they were holding hands as they walked. She was sure the news of them being back together was burning up the gossip lines, and everyone in town would know about it before they reached Berniece's.

Her small farmhouse was just on the outskirts of town. It was only equivalent to a few blocks, but they had to walk down the highway, and a familiar truck slowed as it came toward them.

There were no other cars on the road as the truck stopped, and Dodge poked his head out the window.

"What the heck, Chevy. I know Murphy's old, but are you already looking to upgrade him or are you just test-driving a pet cow?"

"Very funny. Keep driving brother, or you'll get home tonight to find this cow in your bedroom." Chevy waved him on as they both laughed.

Leni had texted her sister when they got close to the library, and Lorna, Elizabeth, Maisie, and all the kids had poured out the doors to pet Babydoll. The cow seemed to eat up the attention, *and* all the apple slices the kids gave her.

But no one was more excited to see Babydoll than Berniece. She was ninety if she was a day, but she practically ran down the porch steps, wavin' and a hollerin' as they were coming up the gravel driveway. She was a tiny thing. Leni guessed she wasn't much taller than five feet, but she still stood up straight in a pressed pink apron over a yellow floral housedress and pink ankle socks with sneakers. She hurried out to greet them and threw her arms around the cow's neck.

"You naughty little thing," she said, scolding the cow. "You had me so worried."

The cow snuggled its big head into her tiny shoulder.

This cow was quite the cuddler.

Berniece hugged the cow one more time then turned to Leni and Chevy. "I've gotten five phone calls from folks telling me you were on your way. I was going to make you some Rice Krispy treats to thank you, but then I saw you were already walking down the highway. I can't thank you enough for bringing my Babydoll home."

"No thanks are necessary, Miss Berniece," Chevy said.

"Oh now, call me Berny. Everybody does."

"All right, Miss Berny. Would you like me to take Babydoll back to the barn for you?"

"Oh, that would be wonderful," Berny told him. "Her stall is the first one on the right. And I'd be much obliged if you filled her water bucket and dumped a half a bale of hay into her trough, while you're in there."

"I'd be happy to," Chevy said, leading the cow toward the barn.

After all the carrots, apples, alfalfa cubes, and geraniums she'd eaten, Leni wasn't sure how hungry the cow was going to be for hay.

She and Berniece made small talk about the weather and the recent thunderstorm and how great it was because they really needed the moisture. Leni had almost forgotten how talking about the much-needed moisture was a staple in any Colorado conversation.

"Now, I want to give you kids a reward," Berny told them when Chevy came back from the barn.

"Oh, there's no need for that," Leni told her.

"Don't sass me," the older woman said, taking two five-dollar bills from her apron pocket and handing them each one. "Now, I want you two to buy yourselves some ice cream. On me. And Babydoll."

Leni started to protest, but Chevy dropped his arm around her shoulder. "We certainly will, Miss Berny. We'll stop at the Tastee Freez on the way home."

"Oh, they have the best chocolate and vanilla twist cones," Berny said.

"Would you like to come with us?" Chevy asked, grinning as he waved his five-dollar bill. "I've got enough for two cones."

Berny stared at him for a moment then an impish grin crossed her face. "You know, I think I will. I usually take a daily walk into town anyway, but I haven't had a handsome fella invite me out for an ice cream in a long time."

Chevy held out his elbow. "Then let's go."

Chapter Twenty-Three

"Did she really walk into town and get ice cream with you?" Mack asked later that night.

He'd made good on his promise and brought sub sandwiches over for supper, even getting a couple for Chevy and himself after Lorna invited them both to stay and eat with them.

Leni knew her sister well enough to know that after they ate, Lorna was going to talk them into staying to play cards or a board game. She loved a good game night.

"She sure did," Leni told him. "Apparently, the woman makes a point to walk two miles a day, so the walk into town was nothing for her. I think she's in better shape than I am. But we had a great time visiting with her while we sat outside the Tastee Freez and ate our ice cream."

"We even got to have ice cream too," Max said, waving around his small ham and cheese sub. "Elizabeth took us to meet them there after the libarary."

"And then we insisted on giving her a ride home," Lorna said. "While Chevy and Leni walked back to the house."

"And I got to see the cow," Max told him. "I wanted to bring her an ice cream too, but Mom said no."

Leni ruffled her nephew's head. "Don't worry, buddy. That cow had already had plenty of treats today."

"Wow," Mack said. "I'd like to meet this Berny. She sounds impressive. And it sounds like quite a day. I'd like to contribute to the conversation, but I spent most of my day mending fence with Ford, and he's not much of a talker."

"No, he is not," Chevy agreed. "But he will talk if he's got something to say."

"Tell us about you," Lorna said, leaning toward Mack. "What was your life like in Texas?"

Mack waved a hand in front of him. "Nah. My life was boring. Never found a cow in my yard. Maybe because we never had any flowers for them to eat. Texas is hot and dry, and that's about all there is to tell." He nodded toward the knee scooter. "How's your leg feeling? You gettin' around on that thing okay?"

"Oh yeah. I still crash into things, but it's so much easier than crutches. And Chevy also brought me a walker from one of his knitting group gals to use around the house, so other than feeling like a ninety-year-old woman, I'm doing great."

"Don't worry. You don't look a day over eighty-three."

She laughed and playfully kicked at him with her good foot.

Mack dodged the kick as he turned to Chevy. "You're in a knitting group?"

Chevy shrugged. "Yes, but it's not as hokey as it sounds."

"He's a terrible knitter," Leni added.

"It was for my grandma," he explained. "It was her group. I started out just giving her a ride into town then she convinced me to come in and say hello and visit a spell. Then I started picking up a couple of her friends on the way, and then…I don't know…when she was gone, I just kept picking up the others and somehow, I became part of the group." He shrugged. "It's fun, and I guess it still makes me feel close to my grandma."

"Sorry man," Mack said. "I wish I could've met her."

"You would've loved her," Chevy said. "Everyone did."

Leni noticed the way Mack had deflected the questions about himself, but maybe he really did think his life was boring and didn't have anything to add to the conversation. He seemed like a good guy—polite, thoughtful, attentive to Max, and kind to everyone, especially Lorna, and he was completely smitten with Izzy—but it wasn't the first time Leni had noticed that he'd redirected the conversation away from himself.

Was he just being a good listener, or did he have something to hide?

Leni wasn't sure.

One thing he couldn't hide was his ineptitude at *Settlers of Catan*. But maybe that's because he was paying too much attention to Lorna and playing a side game of *Candyland* with Max to focus much on his strategy.

"That was a fun night," Leni said, hours later when she was walking Chevy out to his truck.

It was already dark, but the streetlight at the end of the block gave off enough light to see by. Mack had already headed back to the ranch to help with the evening chores, and Lorna was reading to Max while she nursed Izzy before putting them both to bed.

"Yeah, it was," Chevy agreed as he leaned back against the door of his truck and pulled Leni against him to nuzzle her neck. "We could have nights like this all the time…if you stayed."

Her body stiffened, and he noticed, letting out his breath but not letting go of her.

"Sorry. Don't know why I said that. I know you have a life and a job you love in Washington. It just feels awful good having you here." He brushed a lock of hair from her cheek and looked down into her eyes. "And I don't want there to be any doubt or question as to whether I want you to stay. I'm not putting pressure on you or asking you to. It's your decision. I just want you to know that I do. Want you to stay. If you want to."

She didn't say anything—wasn't sure what to say—so she just nodded and pressed a kiss to his lips.

Five minutes later, or maybe it was an hour, it was hard to tell how much time passed when she was wrapped up in Chevy's arms and kissing him, she finally pulled away. "I should probably get back in and check on Lorna."

He opened the truck door and the light from the cab spilled onto the street. "Hey, with all the excitement today, I almost forgot. Murphy bought you something." He pulled a plastic bag from the seat and handed it to her.

"For me?" She opened the bag and pulled out a black T-shirt. Holding it up, she laughed out loud as she read the front. It had a picture of a cowboy hat in the middle surrounded by pink lettering that said, Cowboys & Dirt Make Me a Flirt. "Wow, this is perfect. *Exactly* my style."

"That's what Murphy thought," Chevy said, teasing her since they both knew she would have *never* picked that shirt for herself. "He wanted to replace the one he stole, but there weren't a lot of choices for black shirts at the Mercantile. It was either this or a blue one that said, *Save a Horse, Ride a Cowboy*."

"Always a classic choice."

"Oh, and they had a red one with a rooster on the front that said, *Just a Girl Who Loves Peckers*. Murphy really wanted to get that one. It was a real toss-up, but in the end, we went with the solid black and pink choice. We thought this one seemed the most sophisticated, and that you'd appreciated the way the words rhymed. It felt almost like a poem." He pointed to the shirt. "I mean, that's some cowboy poetry right there."

She laughed harder as she pulled the shirt on over her head, thankful he hadn't chosen the one proclaiming she loved peckers. "It's perfect. I love it. I had no idea your dog had such good taste."

"Yeah, well, he comes by it honestly," Chevy said.

"Tell him thank you. I love it."

And I love you.

She'd almost said the words. They were on the tip of her tongue.

"I'd better get inside. I need to put Max to bed. I'll see you later."

"Call you tomorrow," he said before sneaking in one last kiss.

"Sounds good. I'm at the coffee shop until three."

She went into the house and found Max had already brushed his teeth and put himself to bed. She tucked him in, kissed his forehead then grabbed the load of laundry from the dryer and took the basket into the back room to check on Lorna.

"Nice shirt," her sister said, taking a tiny onesie from the basket as Leni set it between them before dropping onto the edge of the sofa bed.

"Chevy's dog bought it for me. Apparently, it came out of his treat budget since he stole mine the other day at the cabin."

"Makes sense. Although, *you* should have bought that dog a gift. From what you told me, him taking your shirt worked out quite well in your favor."

"True," she said, not able to keep the wicked grin from creasing her face.

"So, how's it going with you two?"

"Good." She let out a sigh as she folded one of Max's shirts that had a Transformer on the front. "I told him I loved the shirt, then I almost told him that I loved *him* too."

"Whoa. That's big. *Do* you love him? Like still? Or maybe again? Or were you just having a knee-jerk reaction to a hot make-out session followed by a cute cowboy giving you a gift?"

"I don't know. I mean this shirt does inspire all

kinds of romantic feelings," she said, pulling out the front of the T-shirt. "But all this stuff, the making out, the *more than* making out, the fun times we have together…I mean we rescued a cow and took an old lady out for ice cream today…how could I *not* be falling in love with him?"

"Oh honey, you might not be able to admit it to yourself, but I'm not sure you've ever *stopped* loving him."

"I'm not sure about that either. But how do I know how much of my feelings are memories from before versus new feelings I have now?"

"What do you think?"

"I think that the boy I loved has seemed to have turned into an amazing man, and I can't stop thinking about him." She stacked another one of Max's T-shirts onto his pile. "This whole day has just been crazy."

"*More* crazy things happened beyond finding a cow in our backyard?"

"Oh yeah. This morning, I took donuts out to the Lassiter ranch to thank the guys for all their help, and when I ask Dodge where Chevy was, he told me that he'd been with Jolene all morning, and that they were still out in the barn together."

"*Jolene*? The girl he left you for that summer after high school?" Lorna crushed the shirt she was folding in her fist. "He was seriously with another girl? *This* morning? I am going to kill him."

"I thought that same thing. And then I found out Jolene wasn't a girl?"

Lorna stopped crushing the shirt and tilted her head at Leni. "Huh?"

"She's a horse. And according to Ford and Duke, a pretty good one."

"Wait. Chevy broke up with you for a *horse*? Like I said, I'm gonna kill him."

Leni gently took the shirt from her sister like it was a loaded weapon. "That's what I thought too. At first." She filled her sister in on everything that had happened that day.

"Wow. You have had a crazy day," Lorna said when she was done. "You had a lot to unpack there, sis."

"There's one more thing," Leni said, her heart racing just thinking about it. "Just now, out by the truck…Chevy asked me to stay. Well, he didn't ask me to *exactly*, but he said he didn't want me to have any doubt that he wanted me to."

Her sister's eyes went wide. "Are you thinking of staying? Because you know you can totally have your old room back. Or we can turn the whole basement into a place for you. I'm just using it to store paper towels and mom's old junk. We can paint it whatever color you want, and we'll get the guys to move your bed and dresser. I know the bathroom down there is outdated, but we could paint the vanity and redo the tile in the shower ourselves. It can't be that hard. And it would be fun to do it together."

Leni held up her hand. "All right, slow down there, HGTV. Don't start watching YouTube videos on how to tile a shower just yet. I committed to staying a few more weeks to help in the shop while your ankle heals, but I never said I was coming back for good. I never even considered it."

"Until now?"

She sighed. "Yeah, until now."

"What about the dream job you just took with NASA?"

Leni folded a pink onesie covered in hearts that read 'Auntie's Little Bestie' and thought about how much she loved being with Max and Izzy and how the job at the space center in Texas would take her so far away from them. "Yeah, I guess I need to figure NASA out."

Chapter Twenty-Four

THE NEXT FEW days flew by, and Chevy barely had a minute to breathe, let alone find time to see Leni. The thunderstorm had done some damage in their pastures, and he and Mack had spent most of the day running and mending fence. He missed her though and thought about her all the time.

She'd been busy at the coffee shop and helping Lorna with the kids, but they'd snuck in a few quick phone calls and had made plans for her to come out to the ranch for dinner that night.

His heart pounded and damned if his palms weren't sweating as he pulled up in front of the house. It had only been a few days, but he couldn't wait to see her, to kiss her, to get his hands on her again.

His lips pulled into a grin as the front door banged open, and Leni came running out and climbed into the truck with him. She had on a pale pink V-neck T-shirt, low top white Converse tennies, and a pair of white shorts that accentuated her tan legs. Her hair was pulled up into a high ponytail, and she wore a smile that was meant just for him.

"Hey there—" he started to say, but she cut him off

with a kiss. Her scent filled the cab of the truck as he slipped his arms around her waist and pulled her across the center console and into his lap. "I've missed you," he told her in between kisses.

"I've missed you too," she said. "Any chance we have time to sneak up to the cabin before supper tonight?"

He chuckled against her mouth, already getting hard just thinking about it. "I wish. But when I told Gramps I was coming into town to get you, he said he needed to grab something at the hardware store and asked to tag along. I just dropped him off, and I think he would notice if it took me an hour to come back and pick him up."

"An hour?" She offered him a naughty grin. "We'd need at least two. Maybe four."

"In that case, how about we skip dessert tonight and head up there right after supper?"

"If you take me to the cabin, you'll still get dessert."

He groaned. "You are killin' me. This is going to be the longest meal of my life." He slipped his hand under her shirt and cupped her breast as he leaned down to graze the top of it with his teeth. "Maybe I'll have my appetizer now."

Leni's phone buzzed in her pocket, and she pulled it out and laughed as she read the screen. "Lorna told us to get a room." She slid back over into the passenger seat and laughed again as her phone buzzed with another message. "And that this is supposed to be a kid-friendly neighborhood."

"Sounds like we'd better get out of here and go get Gramps," Chevy said, adjusting himself before putting the truck in gear.

They parked the truck and met Duke on the sidewalk as he was coming out of the hardware store.

"Let me get that for you, Gramps," Chevy said, taking the bag Duke was carrying.

An old cowboy, dressed in pressed jeans and a short-sleeved, red plaid shirt complete with a longhorn steer bolo tie ambled toward them. He wore a straw cowboy hat and a warm smile as he greeted his grandfather. "Duke, you old so-and-so, how the heck are ya?"

"Hey Buck," Gramps said, returning the man's handshake as he clapped him on the back. "I'm doing fair to midland. Sun's shining, and I've got a brisket in the smoker, so I can't complain too much. You remember my grandson, Chevy," he said, gesturing first Chevy, then to Leni. "And this is Leni Gibbs, Lorna William's older sister. You know Lorna's got that new coffee shop downtown."

"Sure, sure. Great gal," the old cowboy said, shaking each of their hands. "Bucky Ferguson. Good to see you again."

They shared a few pleasantries, mentioned the state of this year's wheat crop, then complained about how dry it had been and how much they needed the moisture.

"Listen Duke, I've been meaning to call you about the guy my son was sending up from Texas," Bucky said, hanging his head. "I'm awful sorry, but it sounds like he's not gonna make it. Dumb idiot took on a bull meaner than him in a roughstock event at last weekend's rodeo. Broke his wrist and fractured his left tibia, so he's not gonna be much use to you, or my son, for this season."

Duke's brow furrowed as he cast a glance at Chevy then back at Bucky. "That's no problem, Buck. Let's hope he has a speedy recovery."

"I'm sure he'll be fine. And probably climbing on the back of another bull by next spring. He's a good cowboy, and a hard worker, but like I said, still a dumb idiot."

"You take care now," Duke told him. "We'll talk soon."

They watched Bucky walk into the hardware store then headed back to the truck. None of them said anything until they were inside the cab.

Chevy put a hand on the steering wheel as he turned to stare at Leni and his grandfather. "If Bucky's guy never showed up, then who the hell is the guy sleeping in Ford's bedroom that I just spent the last two days mending fence with?"

Chapter Twenty-Five

The ride back to the ranch was quiet, both Chevy and his grandfather deep in thought, and Leni letting them be.

Who the hell was this guy?

Was Mack even his real name?

Ford and Elizabeth were sitting at the big, scarred oak table with Mack while Dodge and Maisie were putting together a cutting board full of sliced sausage and cheese in the kitchen when Duke, Chevy, and Leni came into the house. They were all laughing about something but stopped as they took in their subdued expressions.

Murphy got up from his dog bed by the fireplace and came running toward Chevy to rub against his leg. That dog could always read his emotions and must have felt the tension in the room.

Duke strode toward the table, a frown on his normally jovial face as he stared at Mack. "Son, I think you've got some explaining to do."

The color drained from Mack's face. His shoulders fell as he nodded solemnly at Duke. "Yeah, I guess I do."

"What's going on?" Ford asked, his body tensing as he stood and went to his grandfather's side.

"We just ran into Bucky Ferguson outside of the hardware store," Chevy said. "He said the guy his son was sending up from Texas got beat up by a bull last week and isn't going to be able to come up here and help us out this fall."

All eyes turned toward Mack.

"I swear, I didn't mean to deceive anybody," Mack said. "Honestly, when I first got here, Chevy said you all knew I was coming, so I somehow figured you knew who I was. It wasn't until later that I realized you thought I was some guy from Texas sent here to be a farm hand. And by then, I'd spent time with you all, and you'd made me feel like I was already part of the family, and I really liked every one of you." The volume of his voice lowered, and his shoulders fell even further as if the weight of a tractor had been set upon them. "And I guess I just didn't want that to change when you found out who I really was."

"So, who the hell are you?" Ford asked, moving closer to Elizabeth.

Mack's wallet was sitting on the edge of the kitchen counter beside his phone and truck keys, and Dodge grabbed it and flipped it open. "I'll tell you who he is," he said, peering down at the driver's license inside. Then all the color drained from his face as he looked at Mack then at Gramps then at each of his brothers. "Nah," he said, his voice almost a whisper. "You couldn't be."

"What?" Ford said, striding over and snatching the wallet from his brother's hand. "Holy shit," he said, staring down at what Chevy assumed was the guy's license. Ford's face held a mix of hurt and anger as he looked up then waved the wallet at Duke. "Did you know about this? About *him*?"

Chevy stood frozen...anxiety and fear filling his chest. It took a lot to rattle Ford, and his older brother was clearly rattled. Leni took his hand, and he drew strength from having her at his side as he squeezed her palm. "Would somebody please tell me what the ever-lovin' shit is going on?"

Mack sat silent; his head lowered as he stared at a scar on the table.

Ford threw the wallet onto the table. "His driver's license says his name is *Mack Truck* Lassiter."

Chevy jerked his head back. "What the hell kind of name is *Mack Truck*?" Then it hit him, all the pieces falling together. Mack's blue eyes and dark build, so similar to Chevy's. With his free hand, he gripped the back of the chair in front of him to steady himself.

"My dad drove a semi," Mack said quietly, still not looking at any of them. "Or at least that's what she told me. I never met him."

The room was deadly still, as if every person in it were afraid to breathe.

Then Duke let out a weary sigh as he slowly shook his head. His voice was soft and sounded as if every word pained him. "June and I wondered if she might have been pregnant when she left. If that was part of why she'd taken off like she did. We figured it had to do with some new guy she'd met." He sank into the chair in front of him. "She'd gotten a job at the diner out on the highway, so she was either leaving early or coming home late, and we were all busy with the boys and the cattle, so we probably weren't paying enough attention. I remember she seemed to be sick a lot, and she'd put on some weight. But I swear, I didn't know. She never said a word. All these years, she never told us about you."

"She never told me about any of you either." Mack finally looked up at Chevy. "Like you said the first day I met you. Our mother was a real piece of work."

"Wait," Dodge said, the hurt and betrayal plain on his face. "So, you *grew up* with her? She never left you behind?"

Mack huffed out a dry laugh. "In a sense. Yeah, I grew up living with her, but she left me behind plenty of times. She'd take off for days or weeks at a time, sometimes leaving me a fridge and cupboard full of food, sometimes leaving me with nothing but a box of cereal, an expired carton of milk, and a couple of crumpled twenty-dollar bills. We lived in a crappy apartment with more cockroaches than insulation, and I never knew when I woke up in the morning if she was going to be there or not."

Chevy was torn between feeling sorry for the guy and then equally envious and angry at the fact that he still got to grow up with their mother. "But she always came back for you," he said, his lips tight.

"She never came back for us," Dodge said.

"We haven't seen her in decades," Ford added.

From the set of their shoulders and the wary way they were looking at Mack, Chevy knew that his brothers were feeling the same way he was.

"I just found out about you," Mack told them. "She'd gotten a phone call—I think now it might have been from one of you all's dads—then she got sloppy drunk and confessed that I had three half-brothers in Colorado. She said they grew up on a ranch with her parents. She made it sound like it was real nice here. But she told me she'd met a guy, a trucker who came into the diner where she worked, and when she got pregnant with me, he promised her this big life. But I guess he said he couldn't take on four kids, he just wanted to raise his own, so the next time he came through town, she got in his truck with him and left. From what I could gather, she traveled around with him until I was born, then he dumped us in Texas and never came back."

Dodge's brow furrowed as an expression of pain crossed his face. "So, she left *me* behind so she could go off to raise you? I was still in diapers."

Mack looked just as miserable. "I'm sorry."

"Stop," Duke said, slapping his hand on the table. "Don't you *dare* apologize. This is *not your fault*. You were a child. Brandy Lynn is my daughter, and I will always love her, but I'll never understand the way she treated you boys. She was an addict—booze and pills and I don't know what all—so I know she was a prisoner to her addictions. Her mother and I prayed every day that she would break free of those chains, and Lord knows, we did everything we could to help her, but there came a point where we had to let her go and just focus on you boys. But that was on her. It had nothing to do with you boys…" He paused to look each of them in the eye. "You hear me, now? Her deciding to leave was *none* of your faults."

Chevy heard his grandfather's words, but the pain of knowing his mother had cared about alcohol, and herself, more than she'd cared about him, or his brothers, was something he'd lived with his whole life.

Leni still held tight to his hand, offering her silent support as she pressed the side of her body against his.

Duke turned back to Mack, his expression earnest as he focused his attention on him. "I swear, son, if I would known, I would have come for you."

Mack's eyes glistened with tears, but he pressed his lips together as he swallowed and nodded before looking away.

Ford sank back into his chair next to Elizabeth, and she took his hand as he regarded his new half-brother. "Why didn't you just tell us?"

Mack sighed. "I swear I was going to. Every morning when I woke up, I'd swear to myself that I'd come clean and tell you that day, but…"

"But what?" Ford asked, his expression stern. "You decided instead to take advantage of us for one more day?"

"What? No. That was never my intention. And I'm not expecting to get paid or anything for the work I've done here. In fact, I'll even reimburse you for the food I've eaten. I didn't say anything, couldn't tell you, because I've never been part of a family like this before. When I first got here, Chevy said you all had heard that I was coming, so I figured Mom…um, Brandy…must have somehow sent word or called Duke. Then I helped y'all out at the chili festival, and that was one of the best days of my life."

Dodge let out a small huff as if the idea sounded crazy to him.

"I know it probably sounds stupid," Mack went on. "But it's always been just my mom and me. And the older I got and the better I could take care of myself, it was usually just me, sometimes for months at a time. I was always jealous of the other kids at school who had brothers and sisters and families who hung out with each other…eating meals together, going on vacations, or hell, even cleaning out the basement together. That day at the festival, you all took me in and treated me like one of your own. And it was just like I'd imagined a family would be…loud and messy and teasing each other and working together…and that day, I honestly thought you knew who I was and had already accepted me.

"By the time I realized you didn't, I had already imagined myself as part of this family, as a brother and a grandson, and I knew once I told you all the truth, all that would disappear. I'm truly sorry I didn't tell you or that you feel like I deceived you. I never meant to. Honestly, I wasn't trying to hurt anyone." He pushed up from the table, his head hung low as he turned toward the hallway leading to the bedrooms.

"Where are you going?" Duke asked him.

"To pack my stuff," he said. "I can't imagine you want me here now."

Chevy pointed to the empty chair he'd just vacated. "Sit your ass down. That's not how we do things around here."

"Oh." Mack lowered himself back into the chair. "Do you want to take a vote or something?"

"No. This isn't *Survivor*. We're not gonna vote you off the ranch." Chevy looked at Ford then at Dodge, who both gave him small nods. He knew they were all thinking the same thing, and he didn't even have to ask Gramps. "We don't want you to leave. We have some things to work out, sure, but you're our brother, sure as that stupid name confirms, and this ranch has always been the only place we could all call home. Gramps and Gran took us in, no questions asked and treated us like their own. You are family, so this is your home, too."

Mack looked amazed, like he'd just been offered the grand prize in a contest he hadn't known he'd entered. He looked from Chevy to Dodge then to Ford and Duke. "Is that how you all feel?"

Ford, a man of few words anyway, nodded solemnly.

"Course it is, son," Duke said, coming around the table to pull Mack into a bear hug.

Mack looked over at the youngest Lassiter brother. "Dodge? You okay if I stay?"

"'Course," Dodge said, then smiled. "Besides, if you don't stick around, how am I ever gonna get back that ten bucks you owe me for the cheeseburger I got you yesterday?"

That settled it.

So many changes, Chevy thought as he looked down at the woman standing beside him. A new brother. An old love back in his life.

It seemed like for the past several years, his life had felt like he was plodding along a straight dirt road. Sure, he ran into an occasional pothole or bump in the road, but for the most part, his life was a steady mix of ranch work, hanging out with his family, and some random dating here and there.

But now, his life and that road seemed to be full of twists and turns, up hills and down, rain and random forks and choices, and he couldn't wait to see what was up ahead.

Chapter Twenty-Six

IN THE CABIN, later that night, after they'd had their dessert, Leni lay in bed next to Chevy—their naked bodies entwined together—the sheets twisted around their legs.

This felt so good. *He* felt so good. This was what she wanted, this man, this life.

Yes, she had her plants and her favorite Thai food back in Washington, and she had some big changes happening in her career, but this felt like the most important thing to happen to her in a long time.

And she didn't want it to end.

She drew in a deep breath, knowing her next words could change everything, but needing to say them anyway.

Here goes nothing.

And *everything*.

"Hey Chevy, I want to tell you something," she whispered, tipping her face up toward his. "I'm staying here."

"Good," he said, his voice a little drowsy as he pulled her in closer. "I like you here. Let's stay in this bed all night."

"No, Chevy. I mean, I'm staying *here*—in Woodland Hills. I'm moving back in with my sister. She's already offered to remodel the basement. *And* she has it in her head that we're going to learn how to retile the downstairs shower together. I think she's already started picking out tile and paint colors."

He turned on his side, bracing himself up on one elbow as he searched her face. "Are you serious? Are you really thinking about staying?"

She nodded, taking his hand and entwining his fingers with hers. "I've already thought about it. And I've decided. Yes, I'm really staying."

"What about Washington? What about Boeing?"

"That's over. We'll talk more about it, but for now, I want you to know that my life is here now. With you. With Lorna and the kids. I want to really be their aunt. I want to be your girl. I want it all, the late summer skinny-dipping, the fall football games with your crazy brothers, the winter nights curled up in front of the fire. I want to watch my niece and nephew grow up, and I want to do it all with you. I want—"

He cut off her next words with a kiss. A kiss full of promise and a future…and much more dessert.

"She's upstairs in the shower," Lorna told Chevy the next afternoon when he stopped by the house to drop off a plate of sandwiches Duke had put together from the brisket the night before. She was in the kitchen reading a book with Izzy in her lap and her foot up on a chair. "I just heard the water turn on."

"I brought Max a box of Legos, and it should have a bunch of blue ones in it," he told her, setting the box on the table.

"Oh, that's so sweet of you. He'll love them."

"Leni told me his other blue one got thermally reconfigured."

Lorna laughed. "Yes, it was quite traumatic."

"I can imagine. You need anything while I'm here?" he asked as he put the sandwiches in the fridge.

"Nope, I'm good. Elizabeth took Max out for ice cream, and we're about ten minutes away from taking a nap ourselves, so life is good."

Life was good. He was back together with the girl he'd loved and lost, but she was staying this time around, and he couldn't be happier. "You cool if I head upstairs to wait for her?"

"Yep. Just keep it down if you decide to join her. Some of us will be trying to sleep. And don't need the reminder that they haven't had a man in their shower in a very long time."

He chuckled as he bounded up the stairs and into Leni's room. The bathroom door was shut, but he could hear the shower running. He considered shucking off his clothes and climbing in with her, but he might scare the hell out of her if he just yanked back the curtain. Or knowing Leni, she might punch him in the nuts first and ask questions later.

Her bed was neatly made, because she was Leni and had always made her bed, even when they were teenagers, and he sat on the edge of the mattress to wait. In her fastidious way, her room was also neat, no clothes left out or piles on the dresser. Her laptop, a notebook, and a pen were lined up on top of the small desk she'd used when she was a kid.

If the room hadn't been so neat, he might not have noticed, or been inclined to pick up, the folded piece of paper that had fallen to the floor in front of the desk. But he did, and the words at the top of the page caught his eye.

National Aeronautics and Space Administration.

This was a letter from NASA.

He sank back onto the bed. No, this wasn't *just* a letter. This was a letter congratulating Eleanor Gibbs on her acceptance of a position with them. A position that paid more money in one year than he made in five.

And the position she had apparently *already taken* was one she'd been dreaming of her whole life. This job was the whole reason he'd pushed her away the first time—so she would go to college and get this kind of chance to work in the field of space engineering.

But NASA—holy shit.

His heart ached, both at the excitement and pride—he was *so damn proud* of her—and at the heartbreaking realization that he was going to have to push her away again.

Last night she had told him she was staying.

But there was no way in hell he was letting her give this up for him.

The bathroom door opened, and Leni smiled at him as she walked into the bedroom, her hair still wet and dripping onto the shoulders of her robe. Then her smile faltered as she saw his expression…and the letter clutched in his hand.

"NASA?" he whispered, his throat aching as he said the word.

"I was going to tell you—"

"No. What you told me was that you were staying. Here. With me."

"Let me explain—"

He cut her off again. "There's nothing to explain. You got offered a job with NASA—your dream job. I'm not letting you give that up for me."

Her expression changed as her eyes narrowed, and she planted a hand on her hip. "Excuse me? Did you just say you weren't going *to let me* give something up for you? In case you haven't noticed, Chevy Lassiter, I'm not a teenager anymore. I'm a grown-ass woman who can make up her own damn mind. I help build spacecraft, for Pete's sake. I can make my own decisions."

He shook his head. "Not this time."

She lifted her chin. "So, you're pushing me away? Again?"

He stared at her, everything in him wanting to step forward and pull her into his arms, to beg her to stay. But he couldn't. He couldn't ask her to give up her dream. And he couldn't live with himself if she threw her future away—for him.

"Yeah, I guess I am." He dropped the letter on the bed and walked out.

Chapter Twenty-Seven

CHEVY HELD HIS hand up to wave away the dust as his older brother galloped up to him. He'd come home from Leni's and saddled Jolene, intent on losing himself on a trail ride through the mountains behind the ranch. The dark clouds forming in the sky mirrored his gray mood.

"You all right, brother?" Ford asked, pulling his horse up to a stop next to him.

"Yeah, I'm fine," Chevy told him, although he was anything but fine, and the curt tone of his voice wouldn't deter his brother.

"I was running fence and saw you coming across the pasture. You looked so sad, that if you weren't riding her, I'd think your horse must've died. What's got you so down?"

The tightness in his back deflated as his shoulders slumped forward. "Leni got a job offer from NASA."

"Wow. That's amazing. Good for her."

"Yeah, good for her. Bad for me."

"How do you figure?"

"Last night, she told me she'd decided to stay. But I was just at her house and found a letter telling her congratulations on accepting the job. And I can't let her give up a job with fucking NASA, for me."

"Did you tell her that?"

"Damn right I did."

Ford nodded. "Good. Women love it when you tell them what you're gonna *let them* do, or in this case, *not* do."

His brother's sarcasm was not lost on him, and his shoulders drooped lower. "Yeah, that's about the same thing she said."

"So, what happened when you apologized and told her you were wrong to say that?"

Chevy huffed out a dry laugh. "You mean what happened when I pushed her away again and stormed out of her bedroom?"

Ford shook his head. "Ya know, for such a smart guy, you sure can be a dumb ass."

"I know. But seriously, I can't let her give up her dream job, not for me."

"Isn't that for her to decide?"

"I guess, but what if she decides to give it all up—then what am I supposed to do? Just sit around and wait for her to leave me?"

Ford leaned back in his saddle, his brow furrowing as he studied Chevy's face. "So, what's really eatin' at you here? Is this really about her taking a job or is this more about you being afraid she's just gonna leave you anyway?"

Chevy shrugged.

"I get it," Ford told him. "I know that feeling of not being able to trust that somebody is going to stick around for you. And it's probably even stronger right now with just having a new half-brother show up that our mother *did* stick around for…well, sort of, I guess…but my point being is that you can't let what our mother and your shitheel of a father did run roughshod over your entire life. You're a good man, Chevy. And contrary to popular belief, not a total idiot. Do you love this woman or not?"

"You know I do. I've never stopped. You saw how losing her broke my dang heart all those years ago. But that's why I can't watch her throw this chance away. I love her too much. I would do anything for her."

His brother cocked an eyebrow. "Yeah, even risk another broken heart?"

"*Anything.*"

Ford shook his head. "Look, this isn't about her being worth doing anything for. It's about you pulling your head out of your ass and realizing you're worth something too. She obviously loves you. Anyone can see that. And I think we can all agree that Leni Gibbs is one of the smartest people we know, so she wouldn't have told you she was staying if she didn't mean it. You have to trust her too."

"Shit." He leaned forward, resting one arm on the saddlehorn as he scrubbed his hand across the back of his neck. "So, I really screwed this whole thing up, didn't I?"

"Sounds about like it, yeah."

"Guess I need to figure out a way to fix this. I just hope she gives me a chance to tell her what an idiot I was."

Ford pointed to something behind him. "Since

there's only one person I know who drives a fancy blue Tesla, I'd say it looks like your chance is high tailing it down the road right now. If I were you, I'd go catch her."

Chevy turned to see Leni's car kicking up dust on the gravel road—the road that led to the highway.

Aw hell. Had he made her so mad that she was leaving town?

His brother's words had made sense to him. But in that moment of watching the woman he loved driving away from him, he knew that he would do anything to be with her.

He leaned forward, spurring the horse on and she flew across the pasture, almost as if reading his mind and knowing she had to catch the blue car.

"Leni!" he shouted her name as he and the horse galloped up alongside the Tesla.

He didn't know if she heard him yelling through the open sunroof, if she'd caught the motion of the horse next to her, or if maybe she'd just sensed him. Whatever it was, she slowed the car, just as he spotted the downed section of fence Ford had been working on and steered Jolene toward it.

Scattered rain drops hit him in the face as the horse ran through the open section and up onto the road, galloping harder to catch the car.

Leni pulled over onto the shoulder, cut the engine, and opened her door.

The sky opened, and a soft rain started as she stepped out of the car. He galloped up to her and swung out of the saddle. Dropping the reins, he ran to her and swept her into his arms, holding her tight against him as the rain fell onto the dusty road around them.

She looked up at him. "What are you doing?"

"Chasing you down."

"Why?"

"To tell you that I'm an idiot."

She offered him a wry grin. "Tell me something I don't know."

"I will. I'll tell you that I'm in love with you. Still and always. You're the *only one* I've ever loved. And I just got scared."

"I'm scared too. But I know what I want."

"And I know that you've weighed all the pros and cons and that you don't make decisions lightly. And of course, I know that you can make your own choices."

"Yes, I can."

"So, a wise man recently told me…"

"You mean Ford?"

"Well, yeah. How'd you know?"

"I saw him back there in the field."

"Well, he reminded me that I have to trust you, too." The rain was falling lightly around them, but he barely noticed. His attention was all on her, all on the heartfelt declarations he wanted her to hear. "Leni, you are everything to me, and you're worth risking it all for. So, I'm trusting you to make your own decisions, but I want you to know that I'm all in. No matter what you decide. If you stay, we'll make it work. If you take the job and move to Texas, we'll make it work."

She raised an eyebrow. "Come on. Are you sayin' you'd leave Colorado and move to Texas with me?"

"Yeah, I guess that's what I'm sayin', if that's what it takes." He brushed a lock of hair from her wet cheek.

What was it with them and the rain? "I'm trying to tell you that I'm not leaving. And I'm not pushing you away. I'm staying. With you. Wherever you are, I'm going with you. I'm not letting you go again."

Her face broke into a broad grin. "Well, I'm staying, too."

"What about NASA? It's your dream."

"Getting to be with the cowboy I've been in love with for half my life is also my dream. And Chevy, I *can* do both. You're right about me weighing all the pros and cons. And I've already talked it out with my supervisor. I can stay here and work remotely. I just have to fly to Texas to spend a few days in the office each month."

"So, you're really staying?"

"If you'll come with me to Washington to help me pack up my apartment and drive it all back here."

"Hell, yes, I will."

"Then, yeah, I'm really staying."

He pulled her against him, hugging her tight as he captured her mouth in a kiss. She tasted like rain and summer and hope. "I love you, Leni."

"I love you too."

He pulled back to peer down at her, a grin pulling at the corners of his lips. "It's probably a good thing you're going to help build rockets for NASA, because I'm going to love you to the moon and back."

She laughed, a sound he'd never get tired of. "You are a dork."

"Yeah, but I'm your dork."

"Yes, you are. But I have one more question, and it's an important one."

"Ask me anything."

"Any chance you know how to tile a bathroom shower?"

The end…
…and just the beginning…

I HOPE YOU LOVED Chevy and Leni's story. If you want to read what happens on the day Chevy proposes…sign up for my newsletter www.jenniemarts.com. and get the bonus epilogue and a special surprise.

And be sure to preorder Mack's story, LOST AND FOUND COWBOY, the next book in the Lassiter Ranch series, releasing in 2025.

Have you fallen in love with all the cowboys of Lassiter Ranch?

Find the whole series: *www.jenniemarts.com*.

Save the Date for a Cowboy: Prequel Novella to the Lassiter Ranch series
Love at First Cowboy: Book 1
Overdue for a Cowboy: Book 2
Thanks for reading—I write these stories for you!

Be the first to find out when my next books are releasing and hear all the latest news and updates happening by signing up for the Jennie Marts newsletter at: Jenniemarts.com

My biggest thanks goes out to my readers! Thank you for loving my stories and my characters. I would love to invite you to join my street team, Jennie's Page Turners!

Also by Jennie Marts

If you want MORE hot cowboys, meet three brothers who are hockey-playing cowboys in the
Cowboys of Creedence series:
Caught Up in a Cowboy
You Had Me at Cowboy
It Started with a Cowboy
Wish Upon a Cowboy

Even more hunky cowboys can be found in the heartwarming (but still steamy)
Creedence Horse Rescue series:
A Cowboy State of Mind
When a Cowboy Loves a Woman
How to Cowboy
Never Enough Cowboy
Every Bit a Cowboy
A Cowboy Country Christmas

If you enjoy small town contemporary romance with cute cowboys- Try the **Hearts of Montana series:**
Tucked Away
Hidden Away
Stolen Away

If you like hockey romance with cute hockey players and steamy romance-Try the
Bannister Brothers Books:
Icing on the Date
Skirting the Ice
Worth the Shot

More small-town romantic comedy can be found in the
Cotton Creek Romance series:
Romancing the Ranger
Hooked On Love
Catching the Cowgirl

If you love mysteries with humor and romance, be sure to check out **The Page Turners Series** where a group of women in a book club search for clues and romance while eating really great desserts.

Another Saturday Night and I Ain't Got No Body
Easy Like Sunday Mourning
Just Another Maniac Monday
Tangled Up In Tuesday
What To Do About Wednesday
A Halloween Hookup: A Holiday Novella
A Cowboy for Christmas: A Holiday Novella

Even more humor-filled mystery fun can be found in my new **Bee Keeping cozy mystery series**:
Take the Honey and Run
Kill or Bee Killed

Thanks for reading and loving my books!

ABOUT THE AUTHOR

JENNIE MARTS IS the *USA TODAY* Bestselling author of award-winning books filled with love, laughter, and always a happily ever after. Readers call her books "laugh out loud" funny and the "perfect mix of romance, humor, and steam." Fic Central claimed one of her books was "the most fun I've had reading in years."

She is living her own happily ever after in the mountains of Colorado with her husband, two dogs, and a parakeet who loves to tweet to the oldies. She's addicted to Diet Coke, adores Cheetos, and believes you can't have too many books, shoes, or friends.

Her books range from western romance to cozy mysteries, but they all have the charm and appeal of quirky small-town life. She loves genre-mashups like adding romance to her Page Turners cozy mysteries and creating the hockey-playing cowboys

Printed in Great Britain
by Amazon